PUFFIN BOOKS

FURTHER TELEVISION ADVENTURES OF MR MAJEIKA

Mr Majeika is a very special teacher, as Class Three at St Barty's School soon discover. He is a failed wizard from Walpurgis, who has been sent down to Britland. Nothing seems to go right for the lovable and irrepressible Mr Majeika, and hilarious and surprising events are common occurrences at St Barty's.

Humphrey Carpenter is the author of other Mr Majeika books which inspired the television series – *Mr Majeika*, *Mr Majeika and the Music Teacher*, and *Mr Majeika and the Haunted Hotel*, all published in Puffin. He has also written many books for adults and is co-author with his wife, Mari Prichard, of *The Oxford Companion to Children's Literature*. He lives in Oxford and has two children.

D1549818

Other books by Humphrey Carpenter

HUMPHREY CARPENTER

FURTHER TELEVISION
ADVENTURES
——— OF ———
MR MAJEIKA

Based on scripts by Jenny McDade
for the TVS production of 'Mr Majeika'

PUFFIN BOOKS

PUFFIN BOOKS

Published by the Penguin Group
27 Wrights Lane, London W8 5TZ, England
Viking Penguin Inc., 40 West 23rd Street, New York, New York 10010, USA
Penguin Books Australia Ltd, Ringwood, Victoria, Australia
Penguin Books Canada Ltd, 2801 John Street, Markham, Ontario, Canada L3R 1B4
Penguin Books (NZ) Ltd, 182–190 Wairau Road, Auckland 10, New Zealand

Penguin Books Ltd, Registered Offices: Harmondsworth, Middlesex, England

First published 1990
1 3 5 7 9 10 8 6 4 2

Made and printed in Great Britain by
Richard Clay Ltd, Bungay, Suffolk
Filmset in 11/13 pt Palatino

CONTENTS

1

GOODBYE, THOMAS

One tea-time at St Barty's School, in the sleepy village of Much Barty, Mr Majeika was sitting in his classroom trying to catch up on piles and piles of marking.

Mr Majeika was a wizard. Or rather, he was a Failed Wizard. He had failed his Sorcery Exams so often that the Worshipful Wizard had banished him from Walpurgis, the land in the sky where the wizards live. He had sent Mr Majeika down to the very ordinary country of Britland to be a teacher.

Despite the fact that it was meant to be a punishment, most of the time Mr Majeika enjoyed being a teacher. True, there was the marking which took hours and hours and which he hated. He thought that putting an X against something that wasn't quite right wasn't a very kind thing to do. And he hated trying to teach Hamish Bigmore, who was the naughtiest boy in St Barty's School.

But these things didn't matter very much because he had two special friends in Class Three, the class he taught: Thomas Grey and Melanie Brace-Girdle. They were the only children in the school – indeed, they were the only people in the entire village of Much Barty – who knew that

Mr Majeika was secretly a wizard and that he could do magic. The magic sometimes went wrong but that was understandable – he was, after all, a Failed Wizard. Without Thomas and Melanie, things would have been very hard for him. It was very comforting to know that they understood his secret.

Mr Majeika finished marking Hamish Bigmore's arithmetic book – it hadn't taken long, because Hamish had written almost nothing in the book besides some rude words, which were spelt wrong. He was just picking up Thomas Grey's book when there was a knock at the door. 'Come in,' said Mr Majeika.

It was Thomas Grey looking sad and worried. 'Mr Majeika?' he said. 'Can I talk to you for a moment?'

'Of course you can, Thomas,' said Mr Majeika. 'But don't worry. It doesn't matter if you didn't understand all those long division sums I set you today. Between you and me, I don't really understand them myself. In Walpurgis, we never did sums. We just used a crystal ball to tell us the answer.'

'It's not about the maths, Mr Majeika,' said Thomas. 'It's something more important that that.'

'Do you mean the French lessons, Thomas?' said Mr Majeika. 'Don't worry about those either. I'm sure I could find a spell which makes it easier to understand French.'

'No, Mr Majeika,' said Thomas, looking sadder than ever. 'It's nothing to do with lessons at all. It's – well, it's just to say that I'm . . . leaving.'

'Leaving, Thomas?' asked Mr Majeika, puzzled. 'Leaving what?'

'Leaving here,' said Thomas. 'St Barty's School. And Much Barty. You see, Mr Majeika, my parents want me to join them in Africa.' He turned away and gave a gulp.

'Oh,' said Mr Majeika flatly. 'I see.' Then he tried to brighten up a bit. 'Well, of course it'll be lovely to see them again, won't it, Thomas?'

'Yes,' said Thomas, sounding a tiny bit happier. 'But . . .' he went on.

'Yes, Thomas?' said Mr Majeika.

'I don't want to leave *you*, Mr Majeika. And I don't want to leave Melanie, and Mr Potter, and everyone else at St Barty's.'

Mr Majeika's eye was caught by something outside the window. 'Everyone, Thomas?' he asked. 'Come and look out of the window.'

Outside, Hamish Bigmore was fiddling with Mr Majeika's tricycle. This was a very unwise thing to do, because even if Mr Majeika himself hadn't been watching, the tricycle was magic, and was quite capable of giving Hamish a nasty shock all by itself.

But Hamish Bigmore didn't know it was magic. He knew that strange things tended to happen when Mr Majeika was around, but like everyone else at St Barty's (except Thomas and Melanie, of course), he had no idea that Mr Majeika was really a wizard.

Hamish was rooting around in the trike basket to see what he could find. The trike didn't like this; it started to bang its back wheels up and down, like the kicking of an angry horse. But Hamish was so busy prying into the basket he didn't notice. He then found Mr Majeika's magic wand. He didn't know what it was, but because it was so bright and shiny he could see it was something important. So he decided to try and break it.

Hamish sat on the tricycle seat, and started to bash the wand against the trike's bell. Mr Majeika angrily flicked

9

the tuft of hair that stood up in the centre of his head – a sure sign that magic was on the way – and the trike simply disappeared, just like that, leaving Hamish in a heap on the ground.

Thomas squealed with laughter. 'The last time he fiddled with your trike, Mr Majeika, you turned him into a frog.'

'I thought this was a bit less risky,' said Mr Majeika. 'Well, you won't miss Hamish, will you?'

'No,' said Thomas, still laughing. 'I won't miss Hamish Bigmore. But I *will* miss the magic.'

It was two days later, and the school was getting ready to say goodbye to Thomas.

Thomas himself was clearing his things out of Class Three. 'Goodbye, old desk,' he said sadly, giving his desk a pat. 'Goodbye, old tuck box,' he said to the box where he kept his sweets, which was carefully labelled *This Tuck Box belongs to T. P. S. Grey.* (He was leaving it behind as it was too heavy to carry.) He gazed forlornly out of the classroom window to where a sad Melanie was standing by herself in a corner of the playground, while the other children were playing noisily. 'You will look after Melanie, won't you, sir?' he said to Mr Majeika, who was struggling with more marking.

'Of course I will, Thomas,' said Mr Majeika.

'Mr Majeika!' called the voice of Mr Potter, the headmaster. 'The coach is ready!'

Everyone piled into the coach which stood at the school gates – everyone except Hamish Bigmore, who was kicking a stone in the playground.

'Come along, Hamish!' called Mr Potter. 'You want to wave goodbye to Thomas, don't you?'

'I s'pose I'm glad to see him go,' grumbled Hamish. 'Can I have the left-over chocolate from his tuck box?'

'No, you cannot, Hamish,' snorted Mr Potter. 'Now, on to the coach.'

At the railway station, the Barty Majorettes – some local girls in American majorettes' uniforms – were marching up and down, playing a farewell tune for Thomas. It sounded terrible, but Mr Potter thanked them warmly. 'And now,' he called out to everyone as the train pulled in, 'after that unbelievably moving music, it's time for us all to say our goodbyes to Thomas Plantagenet Serlo Grey!'

'Oh, sir!' gasped Thomas. 'Did you have to tell them what all my initials stood for?'

'Thomas,' continued Mr Potter, as Thomas climbed into the train with his luggage, 'has been a part of life at St Barty's School ever since, at the age of three, he joined Miss Flavia Jelley's Painting and Plasticine Class. So, on behalf of all your school friends, Thomas, I would like to take this opportunity of presenting you with a little keepsake.'

Thomas leant out of the train window, and Mr Potter handed him a package wrapped in tissue paper. Thomas opened it and called out delightedly: 'It's a school photograph, everyone!'

They all clapped – all except Hamish Bigmore, who was trying to break into a chocolate machine at the other end of the platform.

'Whenever you look at it, Thomas,' said Mr Potter, 'remember us.'

The guard blew his whistle. 'I will, Mr Potter, I will,' said Thomas. Then he looked closely at the photograph. 'But you're not in it, Mr Majeika!' he called sadly.

Mr Majeika ran up to the carriage window as the train

started to pull out. 'I know, Thomas,' he whispered. 'You see, Walpurgians don't show up in Britlander photographs. That's why I decided to get you a little something of my own.' And he flicked his tuft. Out of nowhere, there appeared in his hand a small package wrapped in black crêpe paper, with a glittery Walpurgian label on it saying 'For Thomas'. He handed it to Thomas.

'Oh, Mr Majeika!' said Thomas. 'Thank you!'

The train was moving faster. Melanie ran alongside, waving and blowing a kiss to Thomas. 'Mummy says we can go out to Africa to see you next year!' she called.

'Don't open that package till you really need it, Thomas,' shouted Mr Majeika. 'Goodbye!'

'Goodbye, Melanie – goodbye, Mr Majeika!' shouted Thomas, leaning out of his window till the train rounded a bend and passed out of sight of Much Barty station. 'And thank you! Thank you!'

'I'm sure Thomas would really *like* me to have the remains of his tuck box, sir,' Hamish Bigmore said to Mr Potter.

'Dear, dear, how we shall miss his . . . er . . .' said Mr Potter to Mr Majeika, when they were back at school.

'His bright smile and his cheery laugh?' suggested Mr Majeika.

'I was thinking more of his termly fees, Majeika,' said Mr Potter, who was doing sums in an account book. 'Crossing T. P. S. Grey off the school list makes quite a large hole in the finances.' He went to the telephone and dialled a number. 'Hello? Is that the Independent Schools' Association? It's the headmaster of St Barty's here. We have a place unexpectedly vacant, which I would be glad to fill as soon as possible. I wonder if you have any suggestions?'

Going out of Mr Potter's study, Mr Majeika ran into Melanie, who was looking miserable. 'Don't worry,' he said to her. 'I know it won't be the same without him. But Mr Potter's trying to find someone else to take his place, so you could land up with an interesting new friend.'

'But there'll never be anyone else like Thomas, Mr Majeika,' said Melanie. 'I shan't talk to the new person – I really shan't, not a word.'

The study door opened, and Mr Potter came out, beaming happily. 'You'll never guess what, Majeika,' he said. 'We've already found a replacement for Thomas. And he's a Prince!'

'I don't care if he is a Prince, Mummy,' Melanie said to her mother, Mrs Bunty Brace-Girdle, when she was at home that evening. 'He's not Thomas and that's what matters.'

'Now, Melanie,' said Mrs Brace-Girdle sharply, 'if you talk like that you'll get smacked legs. It's wonderful that we shall be having Royalty in Much Barty. Which of our dear Queen's family is it to be?'

'Oh no, Mummy,' said Melanie. 'He's not a British Prince. He comes from the East – from the Punjab.'

Mrs Brace-Girdle frowned. 'I hope he'll adjust to the cooler climate. And school meals may pose a problem to someone used to a spicy diet. It won't be easy to make special arrangements for him.'

'Don't be silly, Mummy,' said Melanie. 'I'm sure he'll eat the same food as everyone else. And I'm very glad it isn't a British Prince. I wish Thomas hadn't gone, but if someone has to replace him, it's much more exciting to have a boy

13

from the East. Why,' she continued dreamily, 'he might even know something about magic.'

'Melanie,' said Mrs Brace-Girdle sharply, 'time for bed. And you haven't even finished your maths homework.'

'I don't believe it,' said Hamish Bigmore. 'I bet he's not a real Prince, and I bet he's not richer than my mum and dad.'

'Well,' said Melanie, 'he *is*, so tough luck, Hamish.'

'Of course,' said Mr Potter, looking around Class Three, 'he'll have to have the biggest desk.'

'Naturally, Mr Potter,' said Mr Majeika, helping the head-master to move a large desk to the front of the class.

'Oy!' shouted Hamish Bigmore, who was already in a bad temper because he had raided Thomas's tuck box and found it entirely empty (Thomas had given Melanie the remaining sweets). 'Oy! Whatchoo doing with my desk? I always have the biggest desk.'

'Not any more you don't, Hamish,' said Mr Potter. 'And I wish you hadn't spoiled it by carving your initials all over it.' There was a big *HB* carved with a penknife in the desk-top.

While Mr Potter's back was turned, Mr Majeika flicked his tuft. 'I think it's all right really, Mr Potter,' he said, and pointed at the desk. The *HB* had changed to *HRH*.

'His Royal Highness!' exclaimed Mr Potter. 'How very appropriate! So it wasn't Hamish's initials after all. Really, I must get my eyes tested.' Mr Potter glanced at the row of tuck boxes. They reminded him of something important. 'By the way, Majeika, I ought to have told you. We have received advance notification that His Highness is deeply allergic to chocolate.'

'To chocolate, Mr Potter?' said Mr Majeika.

'Yes, the slightest taste of it makes him feel extremely ill. Under no circumstances must he be allowed to eat any.'

'I quite understand, Mr Potter,' said Mr Majeika.

Hamish Bigmore, who was listening, quite understood too. Already he had a plan to be revenged for the loss of his desk.

The next day, the coach was once again at the school gates, this time to take everybody to the station to welcome the Prince. They all climbed on board – all except Hamish Bigmore, who was nowhere to be seen. 'Perhaps it's just as well, Majeika,' said Mr Potter. 'We don't want any mishaps, do we? Now, I hope everything's ready at the station. We should see the red carpet as soon as we arrive.'

'Is the Prince arriving by magic carpet?' asked Mr Majeika eagerly.

'Of course not, Majeika. We always roll out a red carpet for Royalty. I hope we're going to be in time. I think I can hear the train crossing the Barty Viaduct already.'

The train was indeed crossing the viaduct, and Hamish Bigmore was waiting for it at the side of the line, just behind a signal box. When he saw it coming, he let out a piercing scream, then hid in the bushes.

The signalman came out of his box. 'Who's there?' he called. 'What's the matter?'

Hamish screamed again, and the signalman came running down the steps and began to peer in the bushes. Hamish raced up the steps, ran into the signal box, and pulled all the levers he could find. Then he ran down the stairs again and took to his heels before the signalman noticed that anything was wrong.

As the train approached the signal box, the driver, seeing that the signals had suddenly all gone to 'danger', hurriedly put on his brakes. The train squealed to a halt.

The driver got down from his cab, and went into the signal box, where he found the signalman looking puzzled at the sight of so many levers in the wrong position. Meanwhile, Hamish Bigmore was running along the side of the train.

'That must be him,' he panted, as he saw a door marked 'First Class', and a head in a turban looking out from it. 'Indian Prince bound for St Barty's School?'

'That's right,' called the boy in the turban. 'Who are you?'

'I'm the advance welcoming party, Your Majesty,' grinned Hamish Bigmore.

'It's very puzzling,' Mr Potter was saying to Mr Majeika, as they stood waiting on the platform of Much Barty station. 'I'm sure I heard the train approaching, but there's no sign of it . . . Ah, here it comes now.'

The train was moving slowly round the bend into the station. It drew to a halt, and the door alongside the red carpet was opened. 'This must be him now,' whispered Mr Potter, and he rushed forward and called out, 'Welcome to Much Barty, Your Majesty.'

'Very kind of you, I'm sure,' said the voice of Mrs Fudd, the school cook, who stepped out of the train carrying an armful of smelly cabbages. 'But doncha know, Mr Potter, I'm just plain Missus.'

'Mrs Fudd!' exclaimed Mr Potter. 'But isn't there an Indian Prince on the train?'

'There was some kid with a towel round his head,' said

16

Mrs Fudd. 'But 'e got out just now, up at the signal box. Some bloke opened the door and took him away.'

Mr Potter turned pale. 'Kidnapped!' he gasped to Mr Majeika.

'Pleased to meet you, Prince,' said Hamish Bigmore, holding out his hand. 'Hamish Bigmore's the name. But you can call me Hamish.'

'My name,' said the Indian boy, 'is Samir Chandra Saran Singh. But you can call me Your Royal Highness.' He picked up his suitcase and followed Hamish. 'Where are you taking me?' he asked. 'Why are we climbing through this hole in the hedge?'

'It's a sort of surprise party,' said Hamish, 'to welcome you. It's at the Cherry Tree Tea Rooms, where they sell lots and lots of choc . . . I mean, where the food is terribly good.'

At Much Barty police station, Sergeant Sevenoaks was taking a telephone call. 'You've lost a what, Mr Potter?' he was saying into the receiver. 'Prints, Mr Potter? Prints of what? My auntie had some nice prints of Blackpool that used to hang on her staircase . . . Oh, a prince. A member of Royalty. Last seen on a railway train? Very well, Mr Potter, just leave it to the massed ranks of the Bartyshire Police. I'm sure we'll have him safely back with you in no time.' He put down the receiver.

His colleague P C Pluckley was drinking a cup of tea. 'Massed ranks, Sarge?' he asked, puzzled. 'Who are they?'

'Why, you and me, Pluckley,' said Sergeant Sevenoaks. 'You and me.'

*

In the Cherry Tree Tea Rooms, Hamish Bigmore was giving his order to the waitress. 'For starters,' he said, 'we want a dozen chocolate éclairs, followed by some nice chocolate-coated Black Forest gâteau, and then your entire selection of chocolate fudge cakes. And to wash that down, some really enormous chocolate milk shakes.' The waitress went away to fetch the order.

'Where is the rest of the welcoming party?' asked the Prince. 'And didn't anyone tell you that I'm not supposed to eat chocolate?'

Hamish Bigmore pretended to look shocked. 'Not supposed to eat chocolate, Your Royal Highness?' he gasped. 'Just think what you're missing.' At this moment the waitress turned up with a big plate of éclairs. 'Why, look at it!' said Hamish. 'And think of that delectable choccy taste, that wonderful sticky gooey chocolate slithering down your throat . . .' He stopped. His mouth had begun to water. He grabbed a chocolate éclair and took a big bite. 'Like this,' he said, with his mouth full.

At Much Barty Police Station, the telephone rang again. 'What's that, Mr Potter?' said Sergeant Sevenoaks into the receiver. 'You've lost *another* one? Another Prince, Mr Potter? . . . Oh, just an ordinary boy this time . . . What's his name, Mr Potter? . . . Hamish Bigmore? Now I wouldn't call that boy ordinary, Mr Potter. But you say he's gone missing, Mr Potter? Very well, Mr Potter. I'll put this into the hands of our detective branch, our Criminal Investigation Department. Goodbye, Mr Potter.' He put down the telephone.

'Our what department, Sarge?' asked P C Pluckley, who was drinking another cup of tea.

'Our Criminal Investigation Department, Pluckley. And do you know who that is, Pluckley?'

'No, Sarge.'

'It's you, Pluckley. So get on with it and solve this case, Pluckley.'

'Yes, Sarge ... Let me think, Sarge. Two pupils 'as gone missing, Sarge. Maybe they've both been kidnapped, Sarge.'

'Maybe, Pluckley.'

'But maybe,' and here P C Pluckley's eyes brightened, 'maybe *one of them has kidnapped the other*.'

'Brilliant, Pluckley,' said Sergeant Sevenoaks. 'This could earn you promotion, Pluckley. But you need to find a motive for the crime.'

'Exactly, Sarge,' said PC Pluckley. 'And that's the hard bit. Now, let me think. Why should an Indian Prince want to kidnap Hamish Bigmore?'

'Is it good?' asked the Prince, as he watched Hamish Bigmore eating the last of the chocolate éclairs.

'Oh, fantastic,' spluttered Hamish. 'You really must eat some – I'm sure it won't make you feel ill. Try this chocolate fudge cake.'

'You recommend it?' asked the Prince.

'You bet I do,' said Hamish, stuffing a piece of it into his mouth.

Mr Potter was pacing nervously up and down his study.

'Any news yet, Majeika?' he asked anxiously.

'Not a word, Mr Potter,' said Mr Majeika.

The door opened, and Mrs Pamela Bigmore, Hamish's

mother, collapsed into the room, 'My baby!' she wept. 'Where's my little baby? Isn't there a single trace of him, Mr Potter?'

'Only his satchel, Mrs Bigmore,' said Mr Majeika, picking it up. 'Containing his last night's homework.'

'Incorrectly done,' said Mr Potter.

There was a tap at the study door. Mr Majeika opened it to find Melanie standing outside. 'Couldn't you do something magical, Mr Majeika?' she whispered. 'Isn't there a spell for finding a missing person?'

Mr Majeika thought for a moment. 'I think I remember something of the sort,' he said, and flicked his tuft.

In the Cherry Tree Tea Rooms, Hamish had begun to realize that, though he was stuffing himself with chocolate, the Prince hadn't yet eaten a mouthful. He piled some fudge cake and Black Forest gâteau on to the Prince's plate. 'Do try some,' he said. 'In England, it's frightfully bad manners not to eat something you've been offered.'

The Prince frowned. 'Is it really?' he asked anxiously. 'Well, I don't want to offend you, so perhaps I'll just try a little bit. I'll have to hope it doesn't make me feel poorly.' He put a hand out to take a fudge cake – and at that moment there was a flash and a puff of smoke, and his plate was suddenly empty.

Hamish Bigmore, who was stuffing in more chocolate, looked up. 'Gosh!' he said. 'You ate all that quickly!'

'It hasn't worked, has it?' said Melanie. 'No – wait a minute – what's that on the table? It's just appeared out of nowhere!'

'A plate of chocolate fudge cakes,' said Mr Majeika. 'Now, where have I seen those before?'

'The Cherry Tree Tea Rooms!' said Melanie excitedly. 'But what do you think he's doing there? ... Wait a minute, Mr Majeika. Do you think Hamish Bigmore knows about the Prince and chocolate?'

'I'm sure of it,' said Mr Majeika. 'He was there when Mr Potter warned me about it.'

'In that case,' said Melanie, 'there's not a moment to lose.'

'So, Pluckley,' said Sergeant Sevenoaks. 'Where does the Criminal Investigation Department suggest we go from here?'

P C Pluckley thought for a bit. 'I reckon, Sarge, that we should go to the Cherry Tree Tea Rooms.'

'To look for suspects, Pluckley?'

'No, Sarge, to have tea. They've got scrumptious chocolate fudge cakes, Sarge.'

Hamish was just swallowing the last chocolate fudge cake when Mr Majeika, Melanie, Mr Potter and Pam Bigmore rushed in.

'My baby!' cried Pam.

Hamish's face and hands were covered with chocolate. 'Mummy, I feel sick,' he moaned.

PC Pluckley and Sergeant Sevenoaks were standing disappointedly by the counter. 'No fudge cakes,' grumbled P C Pluckley. 'Just our luck to come here on the day when the fudge cakes have run out.'

'On the other hand,' said Sergeant Sevenoaks, pointing to Hamish Bigmore and the boy who sat opposite him, 'I think the case is solved, Pluckley.'

'Ah,' said PC Pluckley, looking more cheerful. 'That's good, Sarge. Do you reckon I'll get promotion?'

'I shouldn't count on it, Pluckley,' said Sergeant Seven-oaks.

Mr Potter held out his hand to the boy in the turban. 'How do you do, Your Royal Highness?' he said. 'Dudley Cicero Potter, MA (Oxon), DFC, TCP.'

The Prince bowed. 'Samir Chandra Saran Singh,' he said.

'This is Melanie Brace-Girdle,' Mr Potter continued, 'who will be looking after you and helping you to settle in. And this is your teacher, Mr Majeika.'

'I'm so glad you didn't eat any chocolate,' said Melanie.

'I was just going to,' answered the Prince, 'when a strange thing happened. All my chocolate just disappeared in a puff of smoke.'

'Oh?' said Mr Majeika, smiling.

'And do you know,' went on the Prince, 'I once saw something rather like that happen at home. My father, the Maharaja, always had mystic men at his palace who could make strange things happen.'

'You mean,' said Melanie eagerly, 'they were ... magical?'

'I'll say they were!' answered the Prince. 'Especially my favourite teacher, Fakir Safron Poonah.'

'Not Poonah of the Punjab?' gasped Mr Majeika. 'I was at school with him!'

The Prince looked around him, made sure Mr Potter wasn't listening, then whispered to Mr Majeika, 'That means you must be ... Walpurgian!' And he tugged Mr Majeika's nose in a Walpurgian greeting.

'Do you know about Walpurgians, Your Royal Highness?' whispered Melanie.

'Of course,' answered the Prince. 'All students of the

22

mystic arts know about Walpurgis. So if you're a Walpurgian,' he said to Mr Majeika, 'and you're teaching in Much Barty, you must be . . .'

Mr Majeika sighed. 'A Failed Wizard of the Third Class Removed, Your Highness.'

The Prince smiled. 'Don't worry,' he said. 'I can see from the way that plate of chocolate vanished that you know at least as much about magic as did Fakir Poonah. Do you know, I think I'm really going to like it here.'

'I hope so, Your Royal Highness,' said Melanie.

'So do I,' said Mr Majeika, 'Your Royal . . . er . . . Samir . . . er . . . Chandra . . .'

The Prince grinned. 'Just call me Sam,' he said.

Far away from Much Barty, far out to sea, Thomas was lying in the bunk of his cabin, on his way by ship to Africa. He thought sadly of everyone he had left behind, especially Mr Majeika.

Suddenly he remembered Mr Majeika's present. He hadn't even unwrapped it. He got up and searched for it in his coat pocket. There it was, still in its Walpurgian crêpe paper.

Carefully, he untied it. At first it looked like a pocket watch, but when he flipped open the lid he saw it was a photograph of Mr Majeika.

He held it up to look at it closely. It was a very good likeness. 'Goodbye, Mr Majeika,' he said sadly.

'No, Thomas,' said Mr Majeika's voice, and Thomas saw that the photograph of Mr Majeika was wagging its finger at him. 'Not goodbye. We'll meet again soon. And have a safe journey.'

'Thanks, Mr Majeika!' said Thomas happily. And tucking the photograph back in its wrapper, he fell sound asleep.

2

AN INSPECTOR
CALLS

Mr Majeika arrived at school one morning, not long after Prince Sam had taken Thomas's place in Class Three, to find Mr Potter the headmaster looking thoroughly anxious.

'We're going to be inspected, Majeika,' said Mr Potter nervously. 'You know what an Inspection means?'

'Oh yes, Mr Potter,' said Mr Majeika. 'Where I come from, we have Inspections every week. We inspect each other for Bog Fleas.'

'Good gracious,' said Mr Potter. 'Well, Majeika, that's not quite what happens here. It's an Educational Inspection, Majeika. An Inspector comes round to make sure that we teachers are teaching properly.' Mr Potter dabbed his forehead anxiously. 'And to check that we know all the answers to the children's little questions, Majeika.'

'Oh,' said Mr Majeika, suddenly getting anxious himself. Although he had been teaching for several terms, he still knew very little about Britland subjects such as History, Geography and Maths. 'And when will this Inspection take place, Mr Potter?' he asked nervously.

'That's the problem, Majeika,' said Mr Potter in a quavering voice. 'It's today.'

'Today?' gasped Mr Majeika. 'So we've got no time to get ready for it?'

'Scarcely, Majeika,' said Mr Potter. 'The Inspector is arriving after lunch. And if he, or she, decides that we aren't very, very good teachers, Majeika, then St Barty's School will be closed down!'

'I thought you would like to know, Mrs Fudd,' said Mr Potter to the school cook, 'that we are having an Inspection this afternoon, so I hope you will see that everything is clean and tidy.'

''Course I will, Mr Potter,' answered Mrs Fudd. 'Ain't my kitchen always clean an' tidy?'

Mr Potter looked around at the unwashed saucepans, the pans full of greasy water, and the potatoes mouldering in a sack under the sink. He sighed. 'In a manner of speaking, Mrs Fudd, in a manner of speaking . . .'

'Now, if you don't mind, Mr Potter,' said Mrs Fudd, 'I have the Staff Lunch to make.'

'Ah, yes,' said Mr Potter, wincing at the thought of the terrible meals which Mrs Fudd served up every day to himself and the other teachers. 'And what gastronomic delight do you have for us today, Mrs Fudd?'

'Irish Stew, Mr Potter. It's almost ready — would you like a taste?'

'Er, no thank you, Mrs Fudd,' gasped Mr Potter, beating a hasty retreat from the kitchen.

Mrs Fudd looked around for her ladle, to give the Irish Stew a stir. She couldn't find it, so instead she stirred it with an old table-tennis bat that someone had left lying around. She dipped her fingers in, and licked them. 'Mm, not bad,' she said to herself. 'But not quite Irish enough, and it needs a bit more meat.' She uncorked a bottle labelled Irish Whiskey and poured about half of it into the stew. Then she opened a tin of dog food and emptied that in as well. 'Plenty of meat now,' she said to herself.

As usual, Mr Majeika joined the other teachers for the Staff Lunch — and as usual, he opened his packed lunch box and started tucking into his own sandwiches.

'Still bringing your own food, I see, Majeika?' said Mr Potter as he sat down at the head of the table.

'Yes, Mr Potter,' said Mr Majeika. 'I'm afraid I really have to stick to my own diet. Nothing else seems to agree with me.' He bit into a sandwich.

'What is it today, Majeika?' asked Mr Potter. 'Cheese and tomato, or ham and pickle?'

'Not exactly, Mr Potter. In fact it's slug and lovage.'

Mr Potter turned slightly green; and he looked even greener still when Mrs Fudd came through the door from the kitchen, carrying an enormous bowl full of steaming stew. Even at a distance, the smell of her cooking was over-powering.

Several of the teachers began to cough and splutter when they smelt it. 'Rather a strong concoction today, Mrs Fudd,' remarked Mr Potter.

Mrs Fudd eyed him fiercely. 'Then it'll put strength into you, Mr Potter. Now, mind you all eat it up, every scrap, because I don't like to see wasted food, and you shouldn't risk upsetting me, Mr Potter, because if I left, you'd never find another cook like me.'

'You can say that again, Mrs Fudd,' sighed Mr Potter, as

he took a spoonful of the stinking stew, and wished he could hold his nose so as to shut out the awful smell.

Melanie and Prince Sam were eating their packed lunches in Class Three (like most of the children at St Barty's, they couldn't face Mrs Fudd's cooking), when they heard the sound of groaning. They looked out of the window.

One by one, all the teachers — all except Mr Majeika — were coming out of the Staff Room door, moaning and clutching their stomachs. Last of all came Mr Potter, who looked more ill than any of them.

'Oh dear, oh dear,' said Mr Majeika, coming into the classroom. 'I'm afraid none of them are going to be able to teach this afternoon. In fact, I'd guess they'll be off school for a week. And Mr Potter's the worst. She made him have a second helping.'

'Is it Mrs Fudd's cooking?' asked Melanie. Mr Majeika nodded.

Prince Sam laughed. 'And they complain that Indian cooking is strong,' he said. 'So what's going to happen, Mr Majeika?' Mr Majeika sighed. 'Mr Potter's last words to me were, "It's all up to you, Majeika." I've got to look after the whole school.'

'And teach all the classes?' asked Melanie.

'Yes, Melanie, and worse than that, I've got to cope with the Inspector.'

They went downstairs, and Mr Majeika studied the time-table. 'Spanish, Maths, Craft-work, Music Appreciation, French, Projects. How can I teach all these subjects to six different classes at once?'

'You could tell them all to read books quietly to themselves,' said Prince Sam.

'I could, Sam,' said Mr Majeika, 'but the Inspector wouldn't think much of that. We'll just have to hope that he doesn't come after all.'

At that moment there was the sound of wheels in the playground outside. Mr Majeika peered through the front door, then withdrew his head hastily. He looked very pale. 'Oh, no!' he gasped. 'He's here already!'

'How do you know it's him, Mr Majeika?' asked Sam.

'Because his van is labelled *Inspector*!' said Mr Majeika. 'Look, here he comes now!'

Up to the front door came a man in overalls, wearing a bowler hat and carrying a clipboard. An embroidered badge on his overalls read *Inspector*.

'He doesn't look at all the way I thought he would,' whispered Melanie.

'Hush,' whispered Mr Majeika. Then he cleared his throat nervously and said: 'Good afternoon, Your Inspectorship, and welcome to St Barty's.'

''Ullo,' said the man, looking surprised to be addressed like this. Mr Majeika expected him to shake hands, but instead the man got down on his knees and started sniffing in a corner of the entrance hall, making notes on his clipboard.

'There you are!' whispered Mr Majeika. 'He's started inspecting already.'

Sam began to giggle. 'We had an Inspector at my school in India,' he said, 'and he didn't do things a bit like this. But I suppose it's different here.'

'Ssh,' whispered Mr Majeika. Then he said to the Inspector: 'I'm the Acting Head here.'

28

'Oh, yeah?' said the Inspector, who didn't seem interested. He crossed to another corner of the entrance hall and began sniffing there too.

'Perhaps he's got a cold,' whispered Melanie. 'Anyway, Mr Majeika, what are you going to do, with all these classes to teach, and only you to teach them?'

'Won't the Inspector think it strange,' said Sam, 'that we have only one teacher?'

'He certainly will,' whispered Mr Majeika. Then his eyes brightened. 'I've got an idea.' He whispered in Sam and Melanie's ears. They both giggled.

'All right,' said Sam. 'We'll do our best.'

Mr Majeika flicked his tuft, and vanished.

'And this,' said Melanie, opening the door of a classroom and leading the Inspector inside, 'is our Folk Dancing Class.'

The Inspector looked inside. A very old man with a long white beard, dressed in a kilt, was teaching Scottish Dancing to a record of bagpipe music.

'Oh, yeah?' said the Inspector, and began to sniff round the edges of the room.

'Is that really *him*?' whispered Sam to Melanie, pointing at the old man with the beard. Melanie nodded. 'He's done it very well,' whispered Sam. 'But then my old Fakir could change shape too.'

The Inspector seemed to have finished sniffing, so they took him next door to Class Two. 'I hope he's ready,' whispered Melanie to Sam.

When they opened the door, everything was indeed ready. 'Our Needlework Class,' Melanie told the Inspector.

In the middle of Class Two, a tailor was sitting cross-legged on a table, his mouth full of pins, giving instructions to the class. 'That's wonderful,' whispered Sam to Melanie. 'I'd never have recognized him.'

'You can still see his magic tuft of hair,' whispered Melanie. 'Let's hope the Inspector doesn't look too closely.'

But once again, the Inspector wasn't looking at all. He was sniffing in the corners, and he seemed specially interested in a sink that stood near the window. He took out the plug and sniffed carefully down the plughole.

'If that's all you need to see here, Inspector,' Melanie said to him, 'you'd better come next door to our Still Life Class.'

Ten minutes later, Mr Majeika, back in his own shape and clothes, was leaning exhaustedly against the Staff Room door. 'Did I manage it all right?' he whispered to Melanie and Sam.

'Very well indeed,' said Sam. 'Which was the hardest, turning into the Dance Instructor, Art Master, the Tennis Coach, the Recorder Teacher or the Zoologist?'

'They were all exhausting,' panted Mr Majeika. 'But where's the Inspector?'

'Sniffing around the changing rooms,' said Melanie. 'Here he comes.'

The Inspector came downstairs, making notes on his clipboard. 'OK then,' he said. 'Everything seems to be in order.'

'You mean,' said Mr Majeika anxiously, 'that we've passed?'

'Yup,' said the Inspector, looking at the notes he had made. 'All sinks and lavatories clear, no blockages, no bad smells. But I still need to have a look at the old school boiler.'

'Ah,' said Mr Majeika. 'You mean Mrs Fudd?' He took the Inspector into the kitchen, where they found Mrs Fudd cutting up a loaf of stale bread with a saw.

''Ullo, Percy,' she said when she saw the Inspector. 'Back again already? 'Ow time does fly.'

'Do you two know each other?' asked Mr Majeika, amazed.

''Course we does,' said Mrs Fudd. ''E always calls about this time every year, don't you, Percy?'

''Course I does,' said the Inspector. 'Look what it says on me card.' He handed Mr Majeika a small printed card, which said:

> EVERY YEAR
> WITHOUT FEAR
> PERCY STAINES
> WILL CALL ABOUT THE DRAINS
> Tel. Much Barty 222

'*Drains?*' said Mr Majeika faintly. 'You mean, you aren't an Inspector of Schools? Then where on earth has the real Inspector got to?'

The real Inspector had just got off the train at Much Barty station. She was a very fierce-looking, middle-aged lady dressed in blue, carrying a smart briefcase and a furled umbrella. 'Taxi!' she shouted at the top of her voice. 'Taxi!'

Her shouting woke up the Much Barty taxi driver, Piggy Wilson, who was asleep inside his ancient car. He took one look at the owner of the voice, and went back to sleep again.

The woman crossed the station yard and banged on the roof of the taxi with her umbrella. 'I say, you there!' she shouted.

'Wozzat?' said Piggy Wilson sleepily.

'Can you take me to St Barty's School?'

'I can,' said Piggy, 'if I chooses to.' He shut his eyes again.

'Then do so at once,' snapped the woman, getting into the back seat of the car. She got out again quickly with a little scream, for the back seat was already heavily occupied by two piglets, a chicken, some bales of straw, several bags of manure and a coil of barbed wire. 'I can't ride with these,' she screamed at Piggy.

'Please yourself,' said Piggy. 'It's that or walkin', and it's a good two miles.'

Reluctantly, the Inspector climbed in again, keeping the barbed wire between herself and the animals. The pig started to eat her briefcase.

'This taxi is in a disgraceful condition,' she snapped. 'What is that horrible thing doing on the front seat?' She pointed at an enormous fish in a glass case, which, judging from the smell, hadn't been properly preserved or stuffed.

'It's my living, ain't it?' answered Piggy Wilson. He handed the woman a card:

```
┌─────────────────────┐
│                     │
│     P. WILSON       │
│    TAXIDERMIST      │
│                     │
└─────────────────────┘
```

'Do you mean,' groaned Mr Majeika, 'that I've got to go through all this again?'

'It looks like it,' said Melanie. 'Just think of last time as a rehearsal.'

'The real inspector will probably be here at any minute,' said Sam, and it's absolutely vital to put on a good show again. You've done it once, Mr Majeika, so the second time should be easy.'

'But I put so much effort into it,' complained Mr Majeika, 'that I'm quite exhausted. And in any case, back in Walpurgis, when I was studying in Sedementary School for my Sorcery Exams, I never could manage to do the same trick twice. Something always went wrong if I tried it again.'

Now it was Melanie's turn to groan. 'In that case,' she said, 'we'll have to think of something else.'

The taxi drew up at the school gate, and the Inspector got out. 'That'll be two pounds,' said Piggy Wilson.

'Nonsense,' said the Inspector, and gave him a pound.

She pushed open the gate. 'Hinges need oiling,' she muttered to herself. 'Gravel's dirty. And,' she added, reaching the front door, 'there are finger marks on the woodwork.' She rang the bell.

There was a long pause, then Melanie opened the door. 'Are you the Inspector of Schools?' she asked.

'I am,' said the lady Inspector grimly. 'My name is Miss Deirdre Webster-Booth, and the headmaster should be here to greet me.'

'The headmaster is indisposed,' said Prince Sam, appearing at Melanie's side. 'The Acting Head, Mr Majeika, is waiting for you in the headmaster's study.'

They took the Inspector into the study. Mr Majeika got up from Mr Potter's chair and crossed the room nervously to shake hands with her.

'Deirdre Webster-Booth,' said the Inspector, holding out her hand.

Mr Majeika fell over the waste-paper basket. 'Pleased to meet you, Mrs Webbed-Feet,' he said faintly. 'Now, would you like to see around the school? I thought it would be best if, er, these two children conducted you.'

The Inspector raised her eyebrows. 'It's somewhat irregular,' she said, 'but maybe it would be best if you remained in your study, Acting Head. I sometimes find that headmasters and their deputies try to influence my Inspection if they follow me round. They try to make it seem that the school is better run than it really is. I'm glad that you don't want to do that, Mr . . .?'

'Majeika,' said Mr Majeika faintly, sinking back into Mr Potter's chair. 'Off you go then, Melanie and Sam, and take Mrs Wellington-Boot around the school.'

Sam led the Inspector out of the room. 'Good luck, Mr Majeika,' whispered Melanie. 'I'm sure you can do it.'

'I only hope so,' muttered Mr Majeika. Then he shut his eyes, gripped the arms of the chair, and flicked his tuft.

'We thought we'd take you to the Cookery Class first,' explained Sam. 'We have a wonderful French chef – a lady – who does absolutely wizard things with garlic and snails. Absolutely wizard,' he added, giving a slight giggle.

Melanie nudged him in the ribs. 'Ssh!' she whispered. 'Don't give the game away.'

Around the kitchen, which was spick and span, and bore no signs of Mrs Fudd's horrible cooking, stood members of Class Three, dressed in neat white aprons, each of them wearing a small chef's hat. In the middle, somebody in a

34

spotless white uniform, with her own tall hat, was giving a demonstration. She spoke with a strong French accent, but Melanie and Sam could see that she was really Mrs Fudd.

'Now, cheeldren,' she was saying, 'we take ze garlic squeezer, so, an' we squeeze 'im a leetle, an' out comes a leetle drop of garlic, just enough to season ze snail. Ees that OK?'

'No, it's not OK,' said a voice. It was Hamish Bigmore. 'You're not really a French chef, you're –' But Sam's hand closed over Hamish's mouth, and Melanie hastily led the Inspector out of the kitchen.

No sooner had they gone than there was a flash and a puff of smoke – in Mr Potter's study Mr Majeika had flicked his tuft – and everything in the kitchen changed back to normal. Mrs Fudd lost her French accent, her clothes changed to her usual dirty apron, and instead of snails and the garlic squeezer the table was littered with burnt buns. 'Wot are you lot doin' in here?' she shrieked at Class Three. 'Dunno wot's goin' on. I jus' dreamt I was a French chef . . .' Absent-mindedly she chucked the burnt buns into a saucepan of soup, and began to stir it.

'Shall we go to the Music Room next?' Melanie asked the Inspector.

'Certainly, children,' answered Miss Webster-Booth. 'This seems a very unusual school.'

Sam ran on ahead. 'Excuse me,' he said, 'but I have to get ready to sing.'

By the time they got to the music room, Sam was ready at a music stand. He opened his mouth, and at first nothing came out, but then he started to sing – beautifully. 'Oh, for the wings,' he sang, 'for the wings of a dove . . .'

'What a wonderful voice,' said Miss Webster-Booth.

'Yes, indeed,' said Melanie, noticing that Hamish Bigmore had followed them into the room, and was doing something behind a screen. 'Hamish!' she hissed. 'Come out of there!' But it was too late. The record – for a record it was – began to slow down, as Hamish turned off the electricity. Sam's 'voice' started to get lower and lower.

'I'm afraid his voice is breaking more quickly than we expected,' said Melanie. She hustled Miss Webster-Booth out of the room.

Back in Mr Potter's study, Mr Majeika, who had had a rest during the 'music class', was drawing breath for his next piece of magic.

Piggy Wilson was asleep in his taxi by the Much Barty village green, with one of the piglets snoring in his arms. Suddenly there was a *ping*, and he and the piglet vanished.

At that moment, Sam and Melanie were showing Miss Webster-Booth into another classroom. 'This is our Natural History Room,' explained Sam. He opened the door.

In the teacher's chair sat Piggy Wilson, still with the piglet in his arms. He had just woken up, and was trying to make out where he was. Mr Majeika had magicked a teacher's mortar board on to his head, so fortunately Miss Webster-Booth didn't recognize him. But he recognized her.

'Dratted woman owes me a pound,' he muttered. Hastily, Sam and Melanie took the Inspector out into the corridor again.

'Professor Wilson is rather eccentric,' said Melanie, 'but he has constant first-hand contact with animals, and he's an excellent taxidermist.' She shut the door.

'Ah, yes?' said Miss Webster-Booth, wondering why the Professor somehow looked familiar.

'And now,' said Sam, 'our Spanish Class.'

It was a hot afternoon, and Mrs Pamela Bigmore, Hamish's mother, was at home, sitting on her patio with a large cool drink. She had just nodded off to sleep when there was a *ping*, and she, too, vanished.

At the school, Sam and Melanie opened the door of another classroom. Inside, Pam Bigmore, dressed in traditional Spanish costume (Mr Majeika had made a special effort with his tuft to achieve that), was doing a wild dance to an audience of Class Four. 'Arriba! Arriba!' she called as she stamped her feet to the guitar-music (Mr Majeika's gramophone again). 'Flamenco! Flamenco!'

The dance ended, to much applause, and Pam Bigmore sat down in the teacher's chair. 'And now, children,' she asked Class Four, 'what is the first word we learn in Spanish, when we go on holiday there?'

'Very interesting,' murmured Miss Webster-Booth to Melanie. 'But what sort of Spanish is she teaching? Is it Castilian or Latin American?'

'Er, I think it's time we left,' said Melanie hastily. They went out of the room as Pam Bigmore continued the lesson.

'The first word we learn, children,' she was saying, 'is *Oy!* — as in *Oy! Waiter, over 'ere!*'

By this time, Mr Majeika had quite run out of people to magic into teachers, so he decided to take the last class himself. When Sam and Melanie opened the door of Class Five, he was busy teaching basket-work.

'This is our Craft Room,' explained Sam, 'which today is presided over by our Acting Head, Mr Majeika.'

'Tell me, Mr Majeika,' said Miss Webster-Booth, 'which craft do you specialize in?'

'That's right,' said Mr Majeika.

'I asked, which craft?' repeated Miss Webster-Booth.

'Yes,' said Mr Majeika. 'Witch craft.'

'He's simply wizard at everything,' said Sam.

By this time, Mr Potter was feeling better. He struggled out of bed and came over to the school, where he found the Inspector saying goodbye to Melanie and Sam.

Mr Majeika came running up. 'This is Mrs Wet-and-Bossy,' he said to Mr Potter, 'and she thinks the school is marvellous.'

'Ah,' said Mr Potter anxiously, wishing he had stayed in bed after all, 'the Inspector.'

Miss Webster-Booth shook hands with Mr Potter. 'Yes,' she said, 'you have an excellent school, Mr Potter, and I congratulate you. It's absolutely top-hole, and I shall be saying so in my report. In fact, the place seems to run like magic.'

It was tea-time. Piggy Wilson woke up in the back of his taxi, still cradling the piglet, and remembered a strange dream he had had about being a teacher. Pam Bigmore woke up on her patio and remembered that she had dreamt she was doing a Spanish Dance. Mrs Fudd, meanwhile, was getting on with cooking the Staff Supper. 'My, you're looking pleased with yourself, Mr Potter,' she said to the headmaster, as he walked past the kitchen door.

'Yes,' said Mr Potter, 'Majeika's done a wonderful job running the school in my absence. And the Inspector has given us absolutely top rating.'

'That's good,' said Mrs Fudd. 'Well, I've got a special dinner, Mr Potter, so's you can celebrate. One of me best dishes. Stewed bladder of mutton.'

Mr Potter held his hand to his mouth, as if he were about to be sick again. 'That's wonderful, Mrs Fudd,' he said faintly. 'I just can't wait.'

3

MR MAJEIKA'S
HALLOWE'EN

'You haven't forgotten what day it is today, have you, Majeika?'
said the voice of the Worshipful Wizard in Mr Majeika's ear,
just as he was pinning his socks out on the line at the
windmill one morning. Although the land of Walpurgis was
far, far away, up in the sky, Mr Majeika was magically able
to hear the Worshipful Wizard, who ruled Walpurgis, whenever he spoke to him.

'What day, sir?' gasped Mr Majeika, dropping a clothes-
peg. 'I . . . er . . . um . . . that is, sir, I get muddled having to
remember two calendars at once, sir, the Walpurgian and the
Britlander.'

'Well, Majeika,' said the Worshipful Wizard, 'today is the
one day of the year that is the same in both calendars. The thirty-
first of October. And you know what that means, don't you,
Majeika?'

'Um, er, is it Christmas, sir?' asked Mr Majeika, all of a
fluster.

'Don't be absurd, Majeika!' boomed the Worshipful Wizard.
'The thirty-first of October is the most important day in the entire
Walpurgian year — and a pretty important one for Britlanders,
too, especially Britlander bratlings. It's the day when everything

that's grisly and ghastly comes out to play, Majeika. The day when even peaceful little Britland is suddenly filled with witches, ghouls and ghosts, when grim and sinister faces glare out of every window. Yes, Majeika, it's —'

'Hallowe'en, sir!' panted Mr Majeika, throwing himself flat on his face with terror.

He had always found Hallowe'en in Walpurgis utterly terrifying. On that one day in the Walpurgian year, every ghost and ghoul and monster that lurked in the darker, more distant corners of Walpurgis — and the place had plenty of corners that were very dark and distant — was allowed to creep out of its hiding place and roam the passages and staircases and turrets and dungeons, striking terror into the heart of every witch and wizard it met. Mr Majeika always used to go and hide in his wizards' dormitory until it was all over — though even there, nasty things were often lurking under the bed. The thought that Britlanders celebrated Hallowe'en too quite put the wind up him! He decided that, as in Walpurgis, he would hide until it was all over.

He got to his feet, picked up the clothes-pegs, and began to head for the windmill. But it was too late! Already the worst thing imaginable had happened. Waiting for him on the steps of the mill was a ghastly figure such as Mr Majeika had only seen in his worst nightmares!

The figure wore a black coat and a huge black hat, which entirely overshadowed its face. Beneath the hat Mr Majeika could just catch a glimpse of a set of terrible grinning teeth and two luminous green eyes.

'Ex—excuse me, sir?' Mr Majeika whispered to the Worshipful Wizard. 'Are there any of the w—worst m—monsters m—missing from W—Walpurgis at the m—moment?'

'Couldn't say, Majeika,' answered the Worshipful Wizard.

'On Hallowe'en they're allowed to roam where they like. Why, have you found one of them in Britland, Majeika?'

'I th—think so, s—sir,' gasped Mr Majeika, and then he gave a scream, for the terrifying figure was walking towards him.

'Ah, Majeika,' said a familiar voice, as the dreadful figure took off its hat, revealing its ghastly face. 'Just pegging out the washing?'

'Y—yes!' gasped Mr Majeika. 'But w—why do you speak in the v—voice of Mr P—Potter? Have you eaten h—him?'

The figure took off its face. It was Mr Potter, wearing a mask. 'Disguise took you in, eh, Majeika?' he said cheerily.

Mr Majeika sank faintly on to the windmill steps. 'Mr Potter!' he said. 'How could you frighten me like that? Why are you dressed like that, Mr Potter?'

'Hallowe'en, Majeika, Hallowe'en! The day when we all dress up as wizards and witches, ghosts and ghouls. And what will you be dressing up as, Majeika?'

Mr Majeika thought for a moment. 'Well, Mr Potter, I really am dressed up already, aren't I?'

'Are you, Majeika?' said Mr Potter, puzzled. 'As what?'

'Well, Mr Potter, as a Failed Wizard.'

'I don't get the joke,' said Mr Potter, frowning. 'Now, buck up, Majeika, because I need you down at school as quickly as possible, to supervise the children's Hallowe'en costumes. It's one of the biggest events in our school calendar. By the end of today, Majeika, you'll know all about Hallowe'en.'

'I know all about it already, Mr Potter,' said Mr Majeika, feeling rather faint again.

'Motley & Daughter', read the sign on the side of the

furniture van; 'We Buy Junk, We Sell Antiques'. It was parked in a lane a mile or two outside Much Barty.

The crafty-looking man with the red face (Motley) who sat in the driving seat studying a book, and the shady-looking woman in the dirty flower-patterned dress (Daughter) had been to Much Barty before, when they had tried to cheat Mr Majeika at the village jumble sale. They had bought an entire van-load of valuable antique furniture for seven pence, and had hurried off before Mr Majeika discovered his mistake. It was all the worse because the furniture had belonged to Mr Potter and shouldn't have been up for sale anyway. It had taken Mr Majeika all his magic powers to get the furniture back — and to recover Hamish Bigmore, who had been stuck inside a wardrobe that was among the Motleys' van-load.

Lately, times had been hard for the Motleys. All the people in Bartyshire knew them as cheats who gave next to nothing for the stuff they bought from people's houses and cottages, and then tried to sell it for enormous prices. So nobody would sell them anything now, or buy anything from their shop. Therefore the Motleys had decided to turn to burglary.

Mr Motley, sitting in the cab of his van, was studying a book called *Teach Yourself Burglary*. His daughter Felicity was studying a map.

'Good book this, Felicity,' said Mr Motley. 'Tells you 'ow to do it.'

'Good map this, Dad,' said Felicity. 'Shows you where all the rich people's 'ouses are.'

'Oh?' said Mr Motley. 'And where are they?'

'Nearest place to 'ere,' said Felicity, 'is Much Barty.'

*

In Class Three, everyone was fighting over the Hallowe'en costumes. 'Look at me, everyone,' shouted Hamish Bigmore. ''S'me, 's'me who's got the biggest and best.' Mrs Pam Bigmore, of course, had provided her darling son with a very expensive Hallowe'en costume from a London toyshop. But this didn't stop Hamish seizing the last witch's hat from the costume basket.

Mr Majeika saw that a very small girl called Fenella Fudd, the granddaughter of Mrs Fudd the school cook, hadn't got a costume. She was crying quietly in a corner of the classroom. 'What's the matter, Fenella?' he asked her. 'Don't you want to go Trick or Treating with the other children?'

Fenella nodded eagerly. 'But I've got nothing to wear,' she whispered. 'All the costumes seemed so big, I didn't know which one to try, and now there's none left in the basket.'

'Are you sure there's none?' asked Mr Majeika, and taking Fenella's hand, he led her over to the empty costume basket. Flicking his tuft, he bent down and peered inside it. 'Have another look, Fenella,' he whispered.

Fenella peered inside, then gave a scream of delight. 'Ooh, Mr Majeika! There's the best witch costume I've ever seen. And it's just the right size – it's even got my name on it!'

She put on the costume, and the mask that went with it, and everyone told her how good she looked. 'It's splendid,' said Prince Sam.

'Even better than Hamish Bigmore's?' whispered Fenella.

'You bet,' said Sam. 'Just look at Hamish's.' And indeed, expensive though Hamish's costume had been, it was far too big for him. It was a ghost outfit, but he looked completely silly in it. Everyone roared with laughter.

*

At the Barty Barn, Mr Potter was hanging up paper lanterns for the Much Barty Hallowe'en Party. 'Could you pop down to the shop for me, Majeika?' he called when he saw Mr Majeika. 'I'm running out of decorations.'

'Of course, Mr Potter,' said Mr Majeika. 'What sort of decorations do you want?'

'Oh, the usual Hallowe'en things, Majeika. Do hurry up, I have to finish by five o'clock.'

'Very well, Mr Potter,' said Mr Majeika. 'But are you sure people won't be frightened?' He remembered how terrified *he* always was during Hallowe'en in Walpurgis.

'Of course not, Majeika. Now, do hurry.'

Mr Majeika set off for the shop, but it occurred to him that most of the things he needed wouldn't be on sale there anyway. 'Excuse me, sir?' he called to the Worshipful Wizard.

'Yes, Majeika, what is it? Do hurry up – we're trying to finish our Hallowe'en decorations up here.'

'That's just it, sir,' said Mr Majeika. 'Do you think you could spare a few for us down here in Much Barty? You know, sir, the usual sort of thing.'

'Oh, very well, Majeika, we've got a few left over. But do take care of them, and send them back undamaged.'

'Oh, thank you, sir,' said Mr Majeika, as he saw the black balloon already floating down through the sky from Walpurgis, with a large parcel attached to it.

The parcel floated straight into the Barty Barn, and Mr Majeika knew that, being a Walpurgian parcel, it would untie itself on arrival. A moment later he heard a shriek, and Mr Potter ran out of the barn, looking very alarmed.

'Majeika!' he called. 'I think I need to go to the doctor – I've been seeing things!'

'Seeing things, Mr Potter? What sort of things?'

'Skeletons, Majeika, and green slimy things, and giant spiders, and ghastly faces grinning out of nowhere. It must be something I ate – probably Mrs Fudd's school lunch.' He hurried off, looking very green.

Mr Majeika realized that the Walpurgian Hallowe'en decorations were a bit too strong for Much Bartyans. He decided to send them back at once. All they could really cope with in Britland was paper lanterns. 'Thank you, sir,' he called to the Worshipful Wizard, 'but I shan't be needing the parcel after all. So I'm sending it all back – the Brace of Bogeymen, the Double Dose of Demons, the Sackful of Skeletons, the Gaggle of Giant Spiders and the Cackle of Crones.'

'*Thank you, Majeika,*' said the voice of the Worshipful Wizard. '*I'll be glad to have them back – we're running a bit short. And have a good Hallowe'en.*'

'Thank you, sir. And you too, sir.'

Near the village green, Mr Majeika ran into Melanie's mother, Mrs Bunty Brace-Girdle, who was pushing a pram. 'Hello, Mrs Brace-Girdle,' he said. 'Are you going to the Hallowe'en Party tonight?'

'I'm afraid not, Mr Majeika. Not with Baby to look after.' She indicated the pram, which was covered against the cold October weather.

'Baby, Mrs Brace-Girdle?' said Mr Majeika, surprised. 'I had no idea.'

'No idea of what, Mr Majeika?'

'About Baby, Mrs Brace-Girdle. Congratulations! Is it a baby brother or a baby sister for Melanie?'

'Neither, Mr Majeika,' snapped Mrs Brace-Girdle. 'It's not

mine, Mr Majeika. It's Mrs Hebbelthwaite's grandchild. I'm looking after it while its parents have a day out.'

'Ah,' said Mr Majeika. 'I see.' He lifted up one end of the pram cover, but could find nothing underneath.

'The *other* end, Mr Majeika,' said Mrs Brace-Girdle, pointing at the pram hood. Mr Majeika peered in, and saw two eyes and a dribbling mouth.

'And is it a boy or a girl, Mrs Brace-Girdle?' he asked.

'Well, it's wearing blue,' said Mrs Brace-Girdle impatiently. 'That should tell you.'

'Where I come from,' said Mr Majeika, 'babies dressed in blue are Bogies. This isn't a Bogey, is it, Mrs Brace-Girdle?'

'Of course not. It's a little boy. And because I'm looking after it, I shan't be able to go to the party tonight, or take the children round Trick or Treating. Such a pity, but one has to do one's bit for other people, Mr Majeika.'

'Yes,' said Mr Majeika thoughtfully. And then he did a generous thing. 'Would you like *me* to look after Baby, Mrs Brace-Girdle?' he said.

'You, Mr Majeika?' said Mrs Brace-Girdle, astonished. 'Would you really?'

'I'd be delighted,' said Mr Majeika glumly, thinking how sad he was to miss the party. 'Absolutely delighted, Mrs Brace-Girdle.'

'That's fine then. Come to my house at seven o'clock, and I'll show you the ropes.'

'The ropes, Mrs Brace-Girdle? Do you have to tie the baby up with ropes?'

'No, no, just a figure of speech. I'll show you all the things you need for looking after Baby. There are quite a lot of them, you know.'

*

'Dad?'

'Yes, Felicity?'

'Are you sure this is a rich person's house?'

'Sure of it, Felicity. It's marked real big on your map, Felicity, and the name on the gate is "Brace-Girdle". That's what they call a double-barrelled name, Felicity.'

'Oh, yeah, Dad?'

'Yeah. And only the rich have double-barrelled names, Felicity.'

'So that's the house we're going to burgle, is it, Dad?'

'You bet it is, Felicity.'

'Looked after many babies before, have you, Mr Majeika?'

'Not really, Mrs Brace-Girdle,' said Mr Majeika gloomily, looking at the array of nappies, bottles, teats, packets of dried milk, Babygrows and other paraphernalia.

'Well, I expect you'll get the hang of it. You know where to find me, Mr Majeika, if you have any trouble.' And with that, Mrs Brace-Girdle hurried off to the party and left him alone with Baby.

Baby immediately began to cry. And cry and cry and cry.

Mr Majeika picked up one of the bottles and offered it to Baby to suck. Baby pushed it away.

Mr Majeika mixed some baby food with water and put a spoonful of it in Baby's mouth. Baby spat it out, all over Mr Majeika.

Mr Majeika picked up Baby and began to rock it in his arms. Baby's bottom immediately became damp and smelly, and Mr Majeika found that he had got it all over his clothes.

He went to wash it off.

*

'Dad?'

'Yeah, Felicity?'

'Are you sure we need to dress up in these clothes, Dad? These striped jumpers and masks?'

'Well, it's what burglars wear on the films, Felicity. I've seen 'em.'

'It doesn't say nuffink about it in *Teach Yourself Burglary*, Dad.'

'Never mind that, Felicity. It's the uniform, innit? I mean, policemen wear helmets, and burglars wear stripy jumpers and masks. Stands to reason, don't it?'

Mr Majeika was sponging his clothes in Mrs Brace-Girdle's downstairs loo when he saw a face peering in at the window. It was wearing a mask.

He gave a little scream. Then he remembered that Britlanders went around in masks on Hallowe'en. This must be one of them.

He went back into the kitchen where Baby was still crying at the top of its voice. Wrapping it in a blanket, so that it wouldn't make his clothes messy again, he picked it up and began to rock it, singing it a Walpurgian lullaby as he did so:

> *Twinkle, twinkle, little Ghoul,*
> *Shining in your slimy pool,*
> *Rising from the bog so smelly,*
> *Looking like an old green welly,*
> *Twinkle, twinkle, little Ghoul,*
> *Shining in your slimy pool!*

But Baby only went on crying, so Mr Majeika tried again, remembering another song from his childhood, several hundred years ago:

> *Baa, baa, Monster,*
> *Have you any teeth?*
> *'Yes, sir, yes, sir,*
> *Underneath!*
> *Five on my kneecaps,*
> *And ten on my toes,*
> *And many more to eat you up,*
> *Ho ho ho!'*

At this, Baby cried even louder. Suddenly Mr Majeika remembered that Mrs Brace-Girdle had left him a note of instructions. He went into the sitting-room to read it.

'There's someone in the house, Felicity. I saw 'im through the window.'

'I know, Dad. And there's that baby crying. Don't you think we should try another house, where they're all out for the evening?'

'Don't lose yer nerve, Felicity. Remember what it says in *Teach Yourself Burglary*: "If the back part of the house appears to be occupied, break in at the front." Now, take yer rubber mallet, and 'ave a go at that pane of glass by the front door.'

Mr Majeika found Mrs Brace-Girdle's note: 'Baby's parents,' it said, 'will be coming to collect him at about nine o'clock, but they may be a little earlier.' He looked at the clock. It was half past eight. Good, not long to wait. 'Baby probably won't be hungry before then,' the note went on, 'but if he cries, give him some tinned baby food. Follow instructions on tin when warming it up.'

He went back into the kitchen and found a tin. On the side it said: 'Warm contents by standing in hot water for five minutes.' Mr Majeika frowned. It seemed an odd way to warm the food, but Mrs Brace-Girdle had firmly told him to follow the instructions. He filled a basin with hot water, and was just about to take off his shoes and socks and stand in it for five minutes when the front door bell rang.

'Thank goodness!' he sighed. 'That'll be Baby's parents here nice and early.'

'You blithering idiot, Felicity, what you want to go and ring the front doorbell for?'

'It was an accident, Dad. Anyway, it was your fault. You knocked me into the bell after you'd hit yourself with the rubber mallet.'

'Ssh, Felicity, someone's coming.'

The door was opened by Mr Majeika. For a moment he looked surprised to see a man and a woman in striped jumpers and masks. Then he remembered that it was Hallowe'en. 'Oh, I *am* pleased to see you,' he told them.

Motley and Daughter looked at each other. There was nothing in *Teach Yourself Burglary* to prepare them for this. 'You are?' said Mr Motley.

'Of course I am,' said Mr Majeika. 'I know exactly why you're here.'

'You do?' said Felicity nervously.

'Indeed I do,' said Mr Majeika. 'You're here to collect something very precious, aren't you?'

'Well, er,' said Mr Motley, shuffling his feet, 'that's about the size of it.'

'And I'm going to fetch if for you straight away!' said Mr Majeika, hurrying off to fetch Baby.

'Cor,' said Mr Motley. 'Strike me, Felicity, but we've got a right one here. Come to think of it, this is the twerp who sold us that furniture for seven pence. 'E's just the sort of charlie who would give things away to burglars. Open the swag bag, Felicity.'

Mr Majeika came back to the front door clutching a neatly-wrapped bundle. 'Here you are,' he said cheerfully.

'Ta, mate,' said Mr Motley, putting the bundle in his bag. 'Come on, Felicity, run for it!'

When he had tidied up Mrs Brace-Girdle's kitchen, Mr Majeika set off for the Hallowe'en Party. When he got there, he found the whole village having a very jolly time. Those children who weren't out Trick or Treating were bobbing apples in a big tin bath in the corner. Mr Majeika joined in happily, and had just managed to get an apple in his teeth when a fierce voice behind him snapped out his name.

'Mr Majeika! What on earth are *you* doing here?'

Mr Majeika dropped his apple and spun round. 'Oh, Mrs Brace-Girdle,' he said.

'And where is Baby, Mr Majeika?'

'Happily reunited with his parents, Mrs Brace-Girdle. They arrived at your house about ten minutes ago, and took him straight away.'

'Don't be ridiculous, Mr Majeika,' spluttered Mrs Brace-

Girdle. 'Baby's parents are here. I've just been talking to them – they came to the party for a few minutes before collecting Baby. They haven't been to my house to fetch him yet.' She pointed at a young couple on the other side of the barn.

'Are you sure?' asked Mr Majeika, beginning to feel worried. 'They're certainly not the people I gave Baby to.'

Mrs Brace-Girdle's voice rose threateningly. 'And who are the people you gave Baby to, Mr Majeika?'

There was a sudden hush in the barn, as everyone stopped what they were doing and listened.

'Well,' said Mr Majeika, 'they were wearing stripy jumpers and black masks to cover their eyes. And,' he added, remembering something, 'one of them was holding a book called *Teach Yourself Burglary*. So I suppose,' he concluded, 'they must have been . . .'

'Burglars, Mr Majeika,' said Mrs Brace-Girdle. 'You have given Baby to two burglars.'

'Right, Felicity, I'll stop the van here, and we can see what he's given us. Have a look in that blanket. What is it, Felicity? Silver candlesticks? Jewellery? Gold rings and watches?'

'No, Dad. It's a baby.'

'A baby what, Felicity?'

'Just a baby, Dad.'

'Oh, cripes, Felicity. What are we gonna do now?'

'Much Barty Police Station,' said Sergeant Sevenoaks into the receiver. 'What's that, Mrs Brace-Girdle? You've lost a baby? A baby what, Mrs Brace-Girdle? A baby grand piano? A baby Austin? Oh, a baby baby . . . Right, Mrs Brace-Girdle, I'll get the entire force on it right away.' He put down the telephone. 'You 'eard what I said, Pluckley,' he said to the police constable, who was sipping tea. 'The entire force. That means you, Pluckley. On your bike.'

'Right ho, Sarge. What am I looking for this time?'

'A baby, Pluckley. Approximately twenty-three inches tall, no distinguishing marks apart from a lot of dribble around the mouth, and answers to the name of Baby.'

'It's made a mess in its nappy, Dad. I think we ought to change it.'

'Change it, Felicity? What do you reckon we could change it for, some nice silver candlesticks?'

'No, Dad, I meant change its nappy.'

'Let's just get rid of it, Felicity. Let's stop at the next house we come to, and leave it on the doorstep.'

At School Cottage, Mr Potter was just about to take off his Hallowe'en costume when he heard a ring at the bell. He went to the front door, but there was no one there except a baby wrapped in a blanket, lying on the doorstep.

'Good gracious!' said Mr Potter to the baby. 'How on earth did you manage to ring the bell? Oh well, I can't leave you there. We'd better go and see if we can find your mummy.'

*

'Z Victor One to Base,' said PC Pluckley into the phone of the village telephone box, just outside School Cottage.

'Come in, Z Victor One,' said the voice of Sergeant Sevenoaks. 'Any luck yet, Pluckley?'

'No, Sarge. Not a thing . . . Wait a minute, Sarge. There's somebody coming out of that cottage, holding a baby. If I go quietly, I should manage to nab him.'

'Have you heard the latest?' Melanie said to Mr Majeika. 'Mr Potter has been arrested for stealing a baby.'

'Oh, dear,' said Mr Majeika. 'But there must be some mistake. He certainly didn't steal the one I was looking after. I think I'd better do something about this.' He flicked his tuft, and in a few moments his trike had rolled up to the barn all by itself. 'I'm sure the trike can help me find the real thieves,' he explained to Melanie and Prince Sam. 'Anyway, they weren't thieves, because I gave it to them. Quick, trike, take me to them!'

Half an hour later, at the police station, Mr Potter was just being locked into a cell by Sergeant Sevenoaks when there was a commotion at the front of the building. Mr Majeika had arrived with Motley and Daughter, who were handcuffed together and seated on the trike.

'These are the real thieves,' he explained to PC Pluckley, who had come out to see what the noise was, 'only they weren't thieves because they didn't steal it, they were just burglars who happened to come to the front door. I thought they were Baby's parents – it wasn't Mr Potter, so do please let him go.'

'No, we're not thieves, Constable,' said Mr Motley. 'Tell

this bloke to let us go. We're just ordinary honest hard-working burglars — I mean, junk dealers.'

PC Pluckley went to fetch Sergeant Sevenoaks. 'Sarge,' he said, 'there's a bloke out the front with a tricycle, and two burglars on it, but they aren't burglars, they're just junk dealers.'

'Pluckley?'

'Yes, Sarge?'

'Have you had a touch of the sun?'

'No, Sarge.'

'Well, I suppose you're no battier than this bloke in the cells, who says a baby rang his front doorbell. Tell you what, Pluckley . . .'

'Yes, Sarge?'

'Why don't we forget the whole thing, Pluckley? Let them all go, and spend the rest of the evening enjoying ourselves? After all, Pluckley, it is Hallowe'en, and I want to go Trick or Treating.'

'Good idea, Sarge.'

'So, Majeika,' said the voice of the Worshipful Wizard, when Mr Majeika was tucked up in his hammock, just about to go to sleep, *'did you have an exciting Hallowe'en?'*

'Oh yes, sir,' said Mr Majeika exhaustedly.

'Not too dull?'

'Oh no, sir, not dull at all.'

'Because I've been told,' continued the Worshipful Wizard, *'that Hallowe'en in Britland is a very dull thing compared to what we do in Walpurgis. No Braces of Bogeymen, no Double Doses of Demons, no Sackfuls of Skeletons, no Gaggles of Giant Spiders, no Cackles of Crones.'*

'No, sir, none of those things. Just burglars stealing babies — except that they didn't steal it, I gave it to them, and it wasn't Mr Potter's fault, and it was awfully nice of the police to let everyone off, including me, because it was really my fault, and I still don't understand how you warm a tin of baby food by standing in hot water, and I don't ever want to look after a baby again, and next year, sir, please could I come up to Walpurgis, just for the evening, sir, and celebrate Hallowe'en with you, sir, because it'll be a lot more peaceful than it is in Britland.'

4

TROUBLE WITH
TWINS

It was breakfast time, and Mr Majeika was happily munching away at his bowl of Rats Krispies, his favourite Walpurgian cereal, when an envelope was slipped under the door of the windmill. He went and picked it up, and saw it was a Walpurgram – a telegram straight from Walpurgis. He opened it, and read: 'PARCEL ARRIVING – COLLECT IMMEDIATELY.'

'Oh, good,' said Mr Majeika. 'I do like parcels. I wonder if it's a present from one of my Aunties in Walpurgis? But it isn't my birthday, not for ages and ages and ages.' (Walpurgians only have birthdays every forty-seven years.) 'I wonder what it could be?' He hurried off to the village to find out.

At the Much Barty post office, Postman Pulsford was handing out parcels to the ladies of the village. 'Parcel for Miss Palfreyman . . . Parcel for Mrs Phipps . . .' Mr Majeika stood on tiptoe, trying to see if a Walpurgian parcel was sitting on the pile behind the counter.

'You've got a parcel for me, haven't you, Postman Pulsford?' he asked eagerly.

The postman frowned and shook his head. 'No, Mr Majeika, there ain't nothing at all for you today.'

Mr Majeika's face fell. 'Oh,' he said flatly. 'Oh, dear.'

The post office was decorated with French flags, and a big sign said *Bienvenue A Nos Amis*. 'Coming to our celebrations today, Mr Majeika?' asked Postman Pulsford.

'I don't think so,' said Mr Majeika sadly.

'We got them Foreigners coming today, ain't we?' explained Postman Pulsford.

'Have we?' asked Mr Majeika.

'That's right. We get 'em every year. Waste of time, if you ask me.'

Mr Majeika left the post office gloomily when, suddenly, his eye was caught by a black balloon floating down through the sky, with a parcel hanging from it. Of course! Why had he been so stupid as to suppose that a parcel from Walpurgis would arrive at the post office? Walpurgian parcels always came straight down by balloon.

The important thing was to catch them the moment they came to earth, otherwise there was no knowing what mischief might be caused. He got on his trike and pedalled furiously in the direction where the parcel seemed to be landing. And he found himself heading straight back to the windmill.

When he got there, Melanie and Prince Sam were sitting on the steps. They, too, were watching the balloon as it descended gently to earth, released the parcel, and floated back up again.

'Hello, Mr Majeika,' called Sam. 'What do you think it might be?'

'I've no idea,' said Mr Majeika, running to pick it up. Just at that moment he heard the voice of the Worshipful Wizard in his ear, speaking from Walpurgis.

'Morning, Majeika. You're out and about early this morning.'

'That's right, sir.'

'Got something special on today, have we, Majeika?'

'Just your parcel, sir,' said Mr Majeika. 'It's arrived safely, thank you.' He picked up the small parcel, which was wrapped in shiny Walpurgian paper.

'Parcel?' said the Worshipful Wizard. 'What parcel, Majeika? I don't remember sending you any parcel.'

'In that case, sir, it's probably from my Aunty Bubbles, or one of my other aunts.'

'I don't think so, Majeika — they're all away on a trip to the Walpurgian Woods. Are you sure it's from Walpurgis?'

'Absolutely certain, sir.'

'Well, you must have some other friend or admirer up here who's sent you a present. Now, I'm very busy,' concluded the Worshipful Wizard, 'so I'll say goodbye for now, Majeika.'

'Goodbye, sir,' said Mr Majeika, taking the parcel into the windmill and starting to open it.

Melanie and Sam followed him inside. 'What is it?' they asked.

Mr Majeika removed the black crêpe paper that formed the inner wrapping. 'A photograph,' he said. 'A photograph of the Wizards' Graduation Class of '42.'

'1942, Mr Majeika?' asked Sam.

'Oh no, 1842. These are all the young Wizards and Witches — well, they were young then — who graduated with me that year.'

Being a Walpurgian photograph, it floated magically across the room, all by itself, and hung itself up on a picture hook. Mr Majeika gazed at it proudly.

Melanie and Sam examined it closely. About twenty witches and wizards, dressed in gowns and mortar boards, were smiling at the camera. Underneath it said *Sorcery School — Class of '42*.

'Which one is you, Mr Majeika?' asked Melanie.

'That's me – in the bottom left-hand corner.'

'But you're not wearing graduation robes,' said Sam.

Mr Majeika's face fell. 'That's because I hadn't graduated. I was the only wizard in that class who failed.'

Melanie peered more closely at the photograph. 'Wait a minute, Mr Majeika,' she said. 'You *did* graduate after all. Here you are on the other side of the photograph, in your graduation robes. Why are you in the picture twice?'

Mr Majeika peered closely at the picture, then gave a gasp. 'Oh, no, that's not me, Melanie.'

'But it is you, Mr Majeika,' said Sam. 'I'd know your face anywhere.'

'No, Sam,' said Mr Majeika. 'I can understand you and Melanie thinking it's me, because the two of us were incredibly alike. Absolute doubles, identical twins in appearance. We were always getting mistaken for each other. Which was rather unfortunate, because *he* was . . . not a very nice character.'

'Who was he?' asked Melanie eagerly.

Mr Majeika's voice sank to a whisper. 'A certain – Wizard Majolica.'

'And you say he wasn't nice to know?' asked Sam.

Mr Majeika shook his head. 'By no means nice, Sam. In fact, not to put too fine a point on it, he was the wickedest Wizard in the whole of Walpurgis.'

'Golly,' said Melanie. 'A real black Wizard?'

'Absolutely,' said Mr Majeika. 'A complete mischief-maker with no sense of what was right and what was wrong. We could hardly have been more different.'

'But he graduated and you failed,' said Sam. 'So is he still in Walpurgis?'

'No, Sam,' said Mr Majeika. 'They booted him out not long after he graduated, removing his tuft so as to reduce his magic powers. He caused so much trouble that they couldn't possibly let him stay there. He was banished.'

'To Britland, like you?' asked Melanie. 'To become a teacher?'

'Good galaxies, no,' said Mr Majeika.

'You mean,' said Sam, 'that there's an even worse punishment than having to become a teacher, Mr Majeika?'

'Oh, yes,' said Mr Majeika. 'I don't know exactly what happened to him, but I'm sure it was something pretty unpleasant. Anyway, we can be certain that he'll never be allowed into Britland. We're quite safe from him here, children.'

'Are you sure you want his photo hanging here?' asked Melanie.

'Not really,' said Mr Majeika. 'I shan't keep it for long. But I'd like to leave it up for a few days, so I can be reminded of all those nice witches and wizards who were my friends. Now, come along, both of you, or we'll be late for school.'

They left the windmill and went off down the path. Inside the mill, a shaft of sunlight came in through the window and struck the photograph hanging on the wall. If Melanie and Sam had been there to watch, they would have seen the figure of Wizard Majolica, in the corner of the photograph, begin to move.

He peered around him, then, with a horrible cackling laugh, he stepped down from the photograph into the room.

'Aah, there you are, Majeika,' said Mr Potter.

'Good morning, Mr Potter,' said Mr Majeika, staring in

amazement at the headmaster's very curious appearance. He was wearing a striped T-shirt and a beret, and around his neck was a large string of onions. 'Why are you dressed like that, Mr Potter?' he asked.

'Come now,' said Mr Potter, 'surely you haven't forgotten what day it is today, Majeika?'

'Onion Day, Mr Potter?' suggested Mr Majeika.

'Certainly not, Majeika. No, today is the day we celebrate our Twinning, Majeika.'

'Twinning, Mr Potter?' repeated Mr Majeika, who wondered what extraordinary Britland custom he had stumbled across now. 'What is Twinning?'

'Well, Majeika,' said Mr Potter, 'these days every little town and village has its twin, Majeika, just like some people have twins.'

'Ah,' said Mr Majeika, thinking uncomfortably about his own 'twin', Wizard Majolica, and wondering what had happened to him.

(At that moment, in the windmill, Wizard Majolica was taking off his graduation robes and putting on Mr Majeika's spare suit.)

'And we here in Much Barty,' continued Mr Potter, 'are fortunate to have been twinned with a little village in France called Barty-sur-Mer, which translated is "Barty-on-Sea", Majeika.'

'Really, Mr Potter? Is that exciting?'

'Oh yes, Majeika. It means that each year a delegation from Barty-sur-Mer comes over here for the day to celebrate the Twinning.'

'Ah,' said Mr Majeika, remembering what Postman Pulsford had said to him. 'Them Foreigners.'

'Exactly so, Majeika,' said Mr Potter, 'though it's not

quite the way in which I would have expressed it myself. Today, "Them Foreigners", as you put it, will be arriving to partake of traditional English hospitality, here in Much Barty, and to join in the Twinning celebrations. I'm sure they're looking forward to it as much as we are.'

They were not looking forward to it as much as Mr Potter. In fact they were not looking forward to it at all.

'They', the French delegation, 'Them Foreigners' as Postman Pulsford put it, consisted of just two people, the Mayor of Barty-sur-Mer, who was a stout gentleman by the name of Monsieur Claude, and his wife Vinaigrette. They did not enjoy their annual visit to Much Barty in the least.

At this moment, they were eating a picnic of French bread and French cheese, washed down with French wine, on the roadside a mile or two outside Much Barty. The tandem bicycle on which they were travelling rested near them on the grass.

'Pass the good French cheese, my leetle *choufleur*,' Mayor Claude was saying. 'After all, eet ees probably ze last decent zing zat we shall eat today.'

'Too right, *cheri*,' answered Vinaigrette. 'Do you remember, Claude, what ze terrible English gave us to eat last year?'

'All too well, *ma petite*,' groaned Claude. 'Feesh an' sheeps, feesh an' sheeps, nussink but feesh an' sheeps. Oh, 'ow I 'ate their feesh an' sheeps.'

'I thought we'd give them fish and chips again, Majeika,' Mr Potter was saying, as he checked over the arrangements for

64

the Twinning. 'They seemed to like it so much last year. Now, would you please go and check with Mrs Fudd that the food is all ready?'

'Of course, Mr Potter,' said Mr Majeika, and he set off for the school kitchen.

'Melanie and Prince Sam!' called Mr Potter. 'Could you tie those flags up more securely? They've come a bit loose in the wind. Why, Majeika, back already?'

Mr Majeika had indeed appeared at the main door of the school.

'What's wrong?' called Mr Potter. 'Isn't Mrs Fudd ready?'

In reply, Mr Majeika merely giggled in an odd fashion, and then disappeared into the school once more.

A moment later, he was back again. 'Everything's ready, Mr Potter,' he reported. 'Mrs Fudd can have lunch on the table the very moment they arrive.'

'Now, what's going on, Majeika?' spluttered Mr Potter. 'One moment you're here, then you're gone, then you're back again, then you're gone, then you're back again. What are you playing at?'

Mr Majeika frowned. 'I'm sorry, Mr Potter,' he said, 'but I don't understand what you're talking about. I just went to the kitchen to check things with Mrs Fudd, like you said, and then came back again.'

'Oh, well, I must be seeing things,' said Mr Potter. 'Come along, we must finish the preparations.'

Melanie and Sam exchanged puzzled glances. They too had seen Mr Majeika come and go several times. They knew he wouldn't tell a lie to Mr Potter, so what was going on?

Mayor Claude and his wife climbed off their tandem, and

were greeted by the Barty Silver Band playing the French national anthem. 'Welcome, welcome,' called Mr Potter through a microphone. 'And after the rousing strains of that lovely tune, the *Mayonnaise* –'

'*Marseillaise*,' grumbled Mayor Claude.

'– we'll have three rousing cheers to welcome, once again, Them Foreigners – I mean, the splendid delegation from our Twin Village, Barty-sur-Mer.' There was some rather feeble cheering, at the end of which Mr Potter ushered Mayor Claude to the microphone. 'Now,' he said, 'we're going to call on Mayor Claude to make his speech in French, so that our schoolchildren can get some practice in understanding that dreadful – I mean, that delightful language. And for those of us whose French is getting a little rusty, Mrs Bunty Brace-Girdle has kindly consented to act as interpreter and translate Monsieur Claude's speech as he goes along. All ready, Bunty?'

'*Mais oui*, Mr Potter,' said Bunty Brace-Girdle, stepping up to the microphone with a large French dictionary in her hands.

Mr Potter turned to Mayor Claude, speaking to him very loudly and clearly, as if he were deaf. 'It's – time – to – make – your – speech. Speech – speech – you – understand?'

'Of course I understand, Monsieur Potter,' said Mayor Claude irritably. He had been visiting Much Barty every year for ten years, and spoke English better than some of the people who lived there. He cleared his throat and began his French speech.

'*Bonjour*,' he said into the microphone.

Mrs Brace-Girdle thumbled hurriedly through her dictionary. 'Er, I'm not too sure about that one, Mr Potter,' she whispered.

Monsieur Claude continued with his speech. *Je suis Claude, de la Mairie, Barty-sur-Mer.*'

Mrs Brace-Girdle gave her translation. 'I am Mary, a Clod, from Barty-on-Sea.'

'No, no,' hissed Monsieur Claude furiously. 'Zat means "I am from ze Town Hall." Now,' and he continued in French, *'ici ma femme, zis is my wife, qui est une poisonnière.'*

'His wife is a poisoner,' explained Mrs Brace-Girdle.

'Non, non!' screamed Monsieur Claude. *'Poissonière* — she runs a feesh shop.'

'Talking of which,' said Mr Potter, 'it's time for lunch.'

'Don't tell me, let me guess,' said Monsieur Claude. 'We're 'aving feesh an' sheeps?'

'How did you know?' asked Mr Potter.

Melanie and Sam were helping in the kitchen, so they didn't notice anything peculiar going on at lunch. But Mr Potter did.

It was a hot day, and he had already had several glasses of British Sherry, which was what Monsieur Claude and his wife were given each year. (They always poured the sherry away under the table without anyone noticing.) Mr Potter turned to Mr Majeika, who was sitting to his right. 'I think that went off very well, Majeika,' he said.

'Yes, Mr Potter,' said Mr Majeika.

Mr Potter poured himself another glass of sherry, and was just helping himself to more chips when his eye was caught by a something at the other end of the table.

Mr Majeika was sitting there too.

He caught Mr Potter's eye, grinned, raised a glass of sherry to his lips — and vanished! Mr Potter gasped, then turned to his right. Mr Majeika was still sitting there, eating his fish and chips.

'Whatever are you playing at, Majeika?' whispered Mr Potter.

'Playing at, Mr Potter?' answered Mr Majeika, puzzled.

Mr Potter mopped his brow, and as he did so, his eye was caught by someone staring out of a classroom window. *It was Mr Majeika again.* And once more, as Mr Potter watched, he vanished!

Mr Potter stumbled to his feet. 'I'm not feeling too well, Majeika,' he muttered. 'Do you think you could possibly take charge of the proceedings?' And he stumbled off towards School Cottage, mopping his brow.

At that moment, Mrs Fudd arrived with the next course. 'Thought you Frenchies would like some real 'ome cooking,' she shrieked at Monsieur Claude and his wife. 'So 'ere's me own version of that well-known French delicacy, snails 'n' frogs.' She dumped the dish on the table.

Monsieur Claude and his wife looked at it in horror. Mrs Fudd's idea of French cooking was absurd. But Mr Majeika dived into the dish enthusiastically. Snails and frogs was just what they served at the best tables in Walpurgis, and he wasn't going to miss a mouthful!

It was during the performance of French dancing by the Barty Ladies' Can-Can Circle led by Mrs Brace-Girdle that Sam's eye was caught by Mr Majeika. He was sitting at one end of the front row of the audience – and at the other!

Yes, there were definitely two of them. But as Sam's gaze rested first on one, then the other, there was a *ping*, and one of them vanished. 'Melanie,' he whispered, 'I don't think you're going to believe this, but . . .' And he explained what he had seen.

'*Two* Mr Majeikas?' whispered Melanie. 'You're seeing things, Sam . . . unless . . .'

'Yes?' asked Sam.

'That other wizard – the one in the photo. What was his name? Majolica, that's it. Come on, let's run over to the windmill and see.'

Sure enough, when they got to the windmill, the figure of Wizard Majolica was missing from the photograph. 'This is worrying,' said Melanie.

'You bet it is,' said Sam. 'You remember what Mr Majeika said about Wizard Majolica? "The wickedest Wizard in the whole of Walpurgis." And now he's running loose in Much Barty!'

Mr Majeika did not notice anything peculiar until he went on to the stage to announce the next act in the entertainment for the French visitors. 'Ladies and gentlemen,' he said into the microphone, 'we were now to have had a demonstration of handbell ringing by our dear Headmaster, Mr Dudley Cicero Potter. Unfortunately . . .'

As he spoke, he looked along the rows of familiar faces who were watching him from the audience. There, of course, was Mrs Brace-Girdle. There was Mrs Pam Bigmore, upset because Mr Potter had not chosen her dear little son Hamish to give a French recitation. There was Postman Pulsford, and Mrs Fudd, and Miss Haddock, and all the other village ladies. And there was Mr Majeika!

He stopped, frozen in the middle of his announcement, horror-struck at seeing himself sitting in the front row. He stared at the figure, which was his exact double in every way, and was wearing identical clothes. What appalling Walpurgian mistake had he made, that his double should be sitting there, smiling back at him?

Then he noticed that the clothes were not absolutely identical. The suit that the double was wearing had a green stain by one of the pockets, a stain that had been made when Mr Majeika spilled a bowl of bogweed soup during a dinner party in Walpurgis. The double was wearing his second-best suit, the one that usually hung up in a cupboard in the windmill. So he wasn't looking at a mirror-image of himself, but at someone else, who had stolen his suit.

Then he remembered the photograph of Wizard Majolica.

'Unfortunately,' he said into the microphone, 'Mr Potter is indisposed. Instead, Mrs Brace-Girdle will play us *Clair de Lune* on the pianoforte, while I — ' and here his eye was caught by the nasty grin on his double's face '— run away!'

Sam and Melanie were returning from the windmill when they saw Mr Majeika running as fast as his heels would carry him. And after him, not many yards behind, ran the other Mr Majeika.

'Oh, cripes!' said Melanie. 'I'm afraid they're heading for the Barty Boulders.'

'What's that?' asked Sam, as they ran off after the two wizards.

'It's a dangerous rocky place, with a deep drop down to a stream,' said Melanie. 'I'm afraid that one of them could have a nasty fall. And it might be Mr Majeika — the real one!'

Mr Majeika was panting for breath by the time he reached the Boulders. He looked over his shoulder, and could see no sign of his pursuer. With luck, by taking this short cut through the woods, he had managed to shake him off. He leant against a rock, panting and sighing with relief — and found his throat gripped from behind.

'Apprentice Wizard Majeika?' said a voice behind him, a voice he knew all too well.

'Disgraced Wizard Majolica!' he answered. 'But how in Walpurgis did you get here?'

'Who do you think sent you the Sorcery School photograph, eh, Majeika?' hissed Wizard Majolica.

'You mean, it wasn't one of my Aunties?'

'Got it in one, Majeika,' said Wizard Majolica, keeping a tight hold on Mr Majeika's throat. 'As soon as I heard you'd been banished to Britland, Majeika, I sensed that this could be my golden opportunity.'

'Opportunity?' asked Mr Majeika, puzzled.

'Oh,' sneered Wizard Majolica, 'I was forgetting — you never were very bright, were you, Majeika? Failed your Sorcery Exams . . . How many times was it, Majeika? Well, I'll come straight to the point. I'm here to do a deal, Majeika.'

'A deal? What sort of a deal?' asked Mr Majeika nervously.

'A swapping sort of deal,' answered Wizard Majolica. 'You see, you've got everything that I haven't, Majeika. A nice cosy place to hang your hammock — much, much nicer than the Outer Darkness in which I've been living for the past one hundred and eleven years. And then there's your nice little job, Majeika.'

'My job, Wizard Majolica?'

'As a teacher, Majeika. A very cushy little number.'

'Oh, but it isn't always easy,' said Mr Majeika hastily. 'You might not like it at all.'

'Well, it certainly beats re-springing mouse traps,' said Wizard Majolica, 'which is all I've been doing since the Worshipful Wizard threw me out of Walpurgis. And finally, Majeika . . .'

'Yes?' said Mr Majeika brokenly.

'You've got friends, Majeika.'

'Friends, Wizard Majolica?'

'*I've* never had any friends,' said Wizard Majolica.

'I'm not surprised,' said Mr Majeika. 'Who'd be friends with *you*?'

'Quite so, Majeika. But if I swap places with you, I'll have lots of friends, won't I, Majeika? Because all your little friends will think I'm . . . *you*.'

'B–b–but you can't,' spluttered Mr Majeika.

'Oh, can't I?' sneered Wizard Majolica nastily. 'How can you possibly stop me, Majeika? After all, I may have been banished, but I am a Qualified Wizard, while you're just a miserable failure. And now I'm going to prove what a clever Wizard I am, while you're going to fail all over again!'

'He's challenged you to a what, Mr Majeika?' asked Melanie. She and Sam had found Mr Majeika looking white and nervous as he leant against the trunk of a tree overlooking the stream at the Barty Boulders. Wizard Majolica was nowhere to be seen, but judging from a thin plume of smoke emerging from the woods a short distance away, he was making preparations for something.

'A Battle of Spells, children,' explained Mr Majeika. 'Each of us has to try to destroy the other by magic.'

'But you're not qualified to take part in a Battle of Spells,' said Sam. 'You're just a Failed Wizard.'

'I know,' said Mr Majeika miserably. 'But in Walpurgis you must accept a challenge, or forfeit your honour. Of course, if I win, that's the end of Wizard Majolica for ever – we'll never be troubled by him again.'

'And if you lose?' asked Melanie.

'Then I'll be banished to Outer Darkness myself. Oh dear, I think he's calling me now.'

Sure enough, they could hear a voice shouting 'Majeika! Majeika!'

They walked in the direction of the smoke. In a clearing in the wood, Wizard Majolica had made a big ring of fire and smoke. He was standing inside it, summoning Mr Majeika to step into it. 'Oh dear,' said Mr Majeika. 'Wish me luck.'

'But Mr Majeika,' said Sam, 'how shall we know which of you has won? I mean, you both look the same, so how can we tell who's the survivor?'

Mr Majeika thought for a moment, then whispered something in Sam and Melanie's ears. Then he stepped into the magic ring.

Wizard Majolica stepped forward and grabbed Mr Majeika by the tuft of hair on top of his head. He waved his other hand in the air, making a Walpurgian sign. There was a flash and a puff of smoke, and Mr Majeika turned into a bunch of black grapes.

There was another flash and puff, and Wizard Majolica turned into a pair of false teeth. 'Well, Majeika?' said his voice. 'Do I eat you now, or shall we try another spell?'

'You're breaking the rules, Majolica,' came Mr Majeika's voice from the grapes. 'In a Battle of Magic you're supposed to turn *yourself* into creatures or things, not to interfere with your opponent. Like *this*.' As he said these words, the grapes vanished, and their place was taken by a dentist's drill, which began to chase the false teeth round the clearing.

'Well done, Mr Majeika!' cheered Sam. 'Keep up the good work!'

The false teeth vanished, and were replaced by a pair of pliers, which cut the electrical cable of the dentist's drill. It immediately stopped whirring and looked thoroughly broken.

'Oh, no,' gasped Melanie. 'Do you think he's hurt Mr Majeika?'

It seemed very much as if he had, for the dentist's drill vanished, to be replaced by nothing at all. By this time, Wizard Majolica had turned himself into a gorilla, which bounded around the clearing, looking for Mr Majeika. After a few minutes it gave up, and sat down. Immediately it leapt to its feet again, crying out and clutching its bottom.

'It's a drawing pin!' shouted Sam. 'Mr Majeika has turned himself into a drawing pin, and Wizard Majolica has sat on it. Well done, Mr Majeika!'

But Wizard Majolica had recovered his presence of mind. He turned himself into a hammer.

'Oh, no!' gasped Melanie. 'He's going to hammer Mr Majeika into the ground!'

'Wait!' said Sam, pointing at the sky. A black balloon was floating swiftly down. In a moment, it had landed in the clearing, and tied its string tightly around the handle of the hammer. Then it floated up again, carrying the hammer far, far away into the sky, back to Walpurgis.

There was a *ping*, and Mr Majeika appeared beside them again in his proper shape. 'Phew!' he said, wiping his brow. 'That was a narrow squeak.'

'How did you get the balloon to come down, Mr Majeika?' asked Melanie.

'I sent a Walpurgian 999 Emergency Call. That was a Police Balloon, Melanie. It suddenly occurred to me that Wizard Majolica had no right to be in Britland at all, so I got through to the Walpurgian Police and reported an intruder. I don't think we'll be seeing him around here again.'

'Wait a minute,' said Sam. 'You've got to prove that you're the *real* Mr Majeika, and not *him*. Remember what you said?'

'Of course,' said Mr Majeika. 'My tuft. It's a good thing that Majolica lost his when he was banished from Walpurgis, otherwise there'd be absolutely no way of telling the difference between us. Now, let me give it a flick, and by the time we get back to the windmill there should be a really magical tea waiting for us.'

5

HUNT THE
TREASURE

'*Ah, there you are, Majeika,*' said the voice of the Worshipful Wizard one bright and sunny morning, just as Mr Majeika was climbing out of his hammock and rubbing the sleep from his eyes. '*Do you know what day it is up here in Walpurgis?*'

'Er, let me see, sir . . .' said Mr Majeika, trying to remember all the hundred-and-one special days in the Walpurgian calendar. 'Is it Walpurgis Night? Or Hallowe'en again already? Or somebody's birthday?'

'*No, no, Majeika,*' said the Worshipful Wizard impatiently. '*It's Spit and Polish Day!*'

'Is it really, sir?' said Mr Majeika regretfully, for Spit and Polish Day was a very important day indeed, and he was sad to be missing it, down here in Britland.

'*Yes, Majeika, the day upon which we Wizards queue up to have our wands made sparkling by the Wand Polishers. And as you know, we end it all with a most tremendous party.*'

'Of course I know, sir,' said Mr Majeika. 'But there's one thing I've always wondered, sir. Is it true, sir, that you, as Worshipful Wizard, have something else besides your wand, something very special, which also gets polished on this celebrated day? That's what I was always told when I was just a little wizard, sir, and I've never liked to ask.'

The Worshipful Wizard gave a chuckle. *'Didn't know you were so shy, Majeika! Of course there is. There's my Crystal Ball, by means of which I can see everything that's going on all over the world. That gets polished as well today, you know.'*

'Oh, sir, does it, sir? I do wish I could be there to watch. Will I ever qualify for a Crystal Ball, sir?'

'Who can tell, Majeika? Maybe one day, if you ever pass your Sorcery Exams, and then go on to become a Highly Qualified Wizard.'

'A Highly Qualified Wizard,' said Mr Majeika to himself dreamily. Would such a thing ever come to pass? At present, it seemed impossible to imagine that he would ever pass the dreaded Sorcery Exams, let alone reach a higher qualification. Maybe he'd have to spend the rest of his life down here in Britland as a teacher. Still, that wasn't really so bad, and he felt a bit guilty, a bit disloyal to Melanie and Prince Sam, as he stood there dreaming of the higher mysteries of Walpurgian Wizardry.

The voice of the Worshipful Wizard broke in on his thoughts. *'All going well up here, Majeika. My Crystal Ball has just gone off to the Polishers. Should be back in about ten minutes. They bring it back on a cushion, you know, with a lot of ceremony – fanfares of trumpets, and all that sort of thing. I just thought you'd like to know, since these things seem to interest you. Bye for now, Majeika.'*

'Thank you, sir, goodbye for now, sir,' said Mr Majeika sadly, as he ate his breakfast and got ready to go off to school.

He had just done the washing up and was putting on his coat when the Worshipful Wizard's voice could be heard once again. *'Er, Majeika?'*

'Yes, sir?'

'*Thought I ought to let you know, Majeika, that we've got a bit of trouble on our hands up here.*'

'Trouble, sir? What sort of trouble?'

'*It's my Crystal Ball, Majeika. A dreadful thing has happened. It was just being brought back from the Wand Polishers, on its special cushion, with the trumpets playing fanfares, just like I said, when . . .*'

'Yes, sir?'

'*When somebody dropped it, Majeika.*'

'Dropped it, sir? Oh, dear.'

'*Yes, Majeika. Such a thing has never happened before in the annals of Walpurgis. Somebody dropped the Great Crystal Ball.*'

'How awful, sir. Did it break?'

The Worshipful Wizard gave a short laugh. '*Oh no, Majeika. It couldn't possibly break – it was made with an ancient Walpurgian spell which prevents it being broken in any circumstances. No, it didn't break, Majeika, but something almost as bad happened.*'

'What, sir? What in the name of Walpurgis could that be?'

'*Well, Majeika, it was dropped just by the trapdoor which leads out of Walpurgis, and it rolled through the trapdoor and disappeared out of sight.*'

'Oh no, sir, how awful! And do you have any idea where it landed?'

'*Yes, we managed to get a telescope trained on it, and we can see it down there, gleaming away.*'

'That's good news, sir. And where has it landed?'

'*In Britland, Majeika. So it's up to you, Majeika, to recover it and send it back to us as soon as possible. Normal Walpurgian business can't be resumed, you know, until we get it back.*'

'Of course, sir, I quite understand,' said Mr Majeika,

feeling enormously important at being given this vital mission. 'And where exactly has it landed, sir?'

'I've told you already, Majeika,' said the Worshipful Wizard impatiently. 'In Britland.'

'Yes, sir, but where in Britland? It's an awfully big place, sir.'

'Nonsense, Majeika. Britland is nothing like as big as Walpurgis — every Wizard child learns that in Sedementary School. Why, from up here it looks scarcely bigger than a handkerchief. Shouldn't have much trouble finding a Crystal Ball in a place as tiny as that.'

'Oh, but sir,' said Mr Majeika desperately, 'it may look tiny from up there, sir, but that's because you're a long way away. I was teaching Class Three that very thing yesterday, sir, when we were doing Science. If you look at something from a long way away, it appears to be tiny, whereas it may be absolutely enormous.'

'Are you trying to teach me children's stuff?' said the Worshipful Wizard angrily. 'Listen here, Majeika, you're a Failed Wizard, and at present that's the way you're likely to stay. If you want to do yourself a good turn and improve your chances in life, my suggestion is that you go and find that Crystal Ball, and FIND IT NOW!'

'Y—yes, sir, c—certainly, sir, at o—once, sir,' stammered Mr Majeika desperately. 'When you say "Now", sir, do you think you could give me a day or two? It really may take that long, sir.' But there was no reply. The Worshipful Wizard had said his last word on the subject.

'Morning, Majeika,' said Mr Potter as Mr Majeika hurried up to school on his tricycle. 'You're rather late this morning. And you look worried. Anything wrong?'

'Oh no, Mr Potter,' said Mr Majeika. He was late because on the way to school he'd been searching in every hedgerow, every field, every front garden, every dustbin, hoping against hope that he might stumble across the Worshipful Wizard's gleaming treasure, which could have fallen to earth anywhere between Land's End and John-o'-Groat's. (Not that Mr Majeika had heard of those two places, but he knew that Britland was shaped a bit like an old lady driving a car, with the toe at one end and a rather untidy head at the other.) Of course there'd been no sign of it anywhere, and he had already learnt that the inhabitants of Much Barty didn't much care for him poking about in their dustbins and gardens. Clearly the search was going to be very, very difficult.

'Well, Majeika,' said Mr Potter breezily, 'what you need today is a map.'

'A map, Mr Potter? Whatever for?'

'Isn't a map a good idea,' said Mr Potter, 'when you're looking for something precious, that's hidden somewhere around the place, but you don't know exactly where?'

'Why, Mr Potter,' gasped Mr Majeika, 'I had no idea you knew about it.'

'Yes, Majeika,' said Mr Potter, 'today is the day for searching.'

'Absolutely, Mr Potter.'

'Searching for something precious, Majeika, that may be hidden absolutely anywhere.'

'Oh yes, Mr Potter.'

'Something round and shiny, that we've got to find if we're not to lose face entirely.'

'Quite right, Mr Potter. But I still don't understand how you –'

'I'm talking, of course,' said Mr Potter, 'about the Much Barty Treasure Hunt.'

'The – ?' said Mr Majeika, struck dumb.

'The day, Majeika, when each year we compete against the neighbouring village of Barty Porcorum to find the Barty Treasure, a greatly prized trophy, which has been carefully hidden by the Dowager Duchess of Barty. Clues are planted all over the place, and it is our task to unravel them and discover the Treasure before they do. The Treasure Hunt is conducted by car. Have I made myself clear, Majeika?'

'Oh yes, Mr Potter,' said Mr Majeika glumly. He could guess what was coming next. These special days of Mr Potter's always seemed to involve *him* doing all the work.

'This year, Majeika,' went on Mr Potter, 'we anticipate a particularly tough struggle for the Treasure. For many years now, Much Barty has gained an easy victory over Barty Porcorum. But this year, rumours have come to my ears that they are planning to get their revenge. It's not going to be easy, Majeika. I'm appointing you Teacher In Charge Of Treasure-Hunting, Majeika, and I expect results.'

'Yes, Mr Potter.'

'And what's more, Majeika, I expect them fast.'

Mr Potter was absolutely right in suggesting that, this year, Barty Porcorum were out to win the Treasure by fair means or foul. Indeed, they had decided on foul. And the foul means they had chosen involved Hamish Bigmore.

Several weeks ago, Hamish had received a big box of chocolates anonymously through the post. With it was a note that read: 'If you want more of these, then you might try helping your neighbours.' A few days later, Hamish was approached (while out walking his family's Rottweiler dog) by the leader of the Barty Porcorum Treasure Hunt Team, Flying Officer Pongo Fitz-Tightly, an ex-Royal Air Force pilot with a large handlebar moustache, who these days dealt in second-hand Jaguar cars. Flying Officer Pongo made it clear to Hamish Bigmore that if he helped the Barty Porcorum team to win the Treasure this year, he would have a lifetime's supply of chocolates.

Hamish did not take long to make up his mind. In fact, less than half a second.

Now, the traitor to Much Barty was lounging in one of Flying Officer Pongo's best armchairs, stuffing chocolates into his mouth, watched by Flying Officer Pongo and by Flying Officer Pongo's girl-friend, Penelope 'Peaches' Popplewell.

'There he is,' said Flying Officer Pongo, pointing happily at Hamish. 'Barty Porcorum's secret weapon!'

'Really, darling?' drawled Peaches. 'And in what way is he a secret weapon? Frankly, to me he looks like a nauseating little toad.'

Hamish glared at her, pulled out a half-eaten chocolate that he didn't like the taste of, and stuck it on the hem of Peaches' dress. She gave a little scream.

'Anyway,' she drawled, 'secret weapon or no secret weapon, if you ask me it's all just plain cheating.'

Flying Officer Pongo stuck a cigarette into the end of his holder and lit it. 'Let's just call it Insider Dealing, shall we? Now, Hamish, what I want you to do is this . . .'

In the Barty Woods, the Dowager Duchess had arrived to

bury the Barty Treasure. An elaborate ceremony was taking place.

Having been pushed to a suitable spot in her wheelchair, the old lady gave a nod to her footman, who removed from his own head the ceremonial Treasure Hunt Cap, with its shovel-shaped peak, carefully reinforced with steel. He then knelt on one knee and began to scrape away the soil until a sizeable hole had been made in the ground.

The Dowager Duchess's nurse now took from a velvet-covered box a round object that could be seen gleaming beneath its cloth of chamois-leather. This was the celebrated Barty Treasure itself, donated by the Dowager Duchess's father as long ago as 1926, and competed for every year since then.

Carefully, the footman placed the Treasure in the hole in the ground and then covered it again with earth so that nothing was to be seen of the hiding place.

He then rose to his feet and pinned to the nearest tree the first of a series of green envelopes containing the clues that would help the winning team to reach its prize. 'All done, Your Grace,' he mumbled to the Dowager Duchess.

'You've forgotten something, Stiggins,' snapped the old lady. 'What about the flag?'

Muttering an apology, the footman took from his bag a small flag on a stick, bearing the Duke of Barty's crest, and carefully stuck this into the ground to mark the spot where the Treasure was buried.

This final ritual being completed, the party set off again for the waiting car that would take the Dowager Duchess back to Barty Towers.

Meanwhile, in the branches of an oak tree not far from the spot where the Barty Treasure was buried, the sunlight caught something exceptionally shiny and glinting that had fallen from the sky an hour or two earlier.

It was the Worshipful Wizard's Crystal Ball.

'But Mr Majeika,' said Prince Sam, when Mr Majeika had explained the problem to him and Melanie, 'surely you could just flick your tuft and find the Crystal Ball by magic, like you found Hamish Bigmore giving me chocolate in the Tea Rooms?'

'It's not as simple as that, Sam,' sighed Mr Majeika. 'Magic can't easily be used against magic. If the Crystal Ball was just any old crystal ball, I'm sure I could. But magical things have a way of resisting spells. Still, let's try it. I'll make a spell to summon any round and shiny thing that can be seen for twenty miles around. You never know what might turn up.'

He thought hard for a moment, then flicked his tuft. There was a sudden commotion, and the classroom became filled with goldfish bowls, motorcycle helmets, glass lampshades, a fruit bowl belonging to Mrs Fudd containing some very nasty-looking suet pudding and a cut-glass dish that Mr Potter's auntie had sent him from Bognor Regis.

'Oh, dear,' sighed Mr Majeika, as he sent the whole lot back again by magic. 'You see what I mean?'

'All ready, Hamish?' asked Flying Officer Pongo.

'Yup,' said Hamish through a mouthful of chocolates.

'Got the packet of drawing pins to puncture the tyres of the Much Barty car? The false clues to plant all over the place? The can of dirty oil to spread on the road so that the car skids all over the place?'

'Yup,' said Hamish, stuffing more chocolates into his mouth.

'I hope you've put the oil somewhere safe,' said Flying Officer Pongo. 'The can was leaking, and we don't want it anywhere near our clothes.'

'It's on the back seat of your car,' mumbled Hamish. '*She's* sitting next to it.'

Peaches Popplewell gave a little shriek and leapt from her seat in the back of the car. 'My dress! My dress! It's got oil all over it! He's absolutely ruined my dress, the little toad.'

'I've got an idea,' said Prince Sam. 'Don't you often use your trike, Mr Majeika, to find things or people that have disappeared?'

Mr Majeika nodded.

'Well then,' said Sam, 'why not try it now?'

'Yes,' said Melanie. 'It doesn't usually make mistakes with magic the way you do.'

'That's not a very kind way of putting it,' said Mr Majeika. 'But you may be right.' He whistled for the trike and it came rolling up to the main door of the school. Mr Majeika whispered something to it, then flicked his tuft, then got on and let the trike carry him where it wanted.

It sped off in the direction of the Barty Woods.

Only twenty minutes later, it was back again, with Mr Majeika looking absolutely delighted. 'That was a brilliant idea, Sam,' he said. 'The trike took me straight to the spot.'

'You found the Crystal Ball?' asked Melanie.

'With the greatest of ease,' explained Mr Majeika.

'Where was it?' asked Sam. 'In the branches of a tree, or lying on the ground?'

'Neither,' said Mr Majeika. 'It must have fallen to earth very hard, because it was actually buried under some loose soil. The funny thing was, someone had marked the spot with a little flag.'

'Goodness,' said Melanie. 'Who do you think would have done that?'

'I can't imagine,' said Mr Majeika. 'Perhaps the Worshipful Wizard has been sending other people to look for it — though I don't understand why anyone who knew where it was didn't send it back at once.'

'And did you send it back?' asked Sam.

'Oh yes, straight away. I only had to throw it up into the sky and off it went towards Walpurgis. I'm sure the Worshipful Wizard has got it safely back by now.'

The Worshipful Wizard had indeed received the round shiny object that Mr Majeika had thrown up into the sky and had sent it straight off to Wizard Spit, the Chief Wand Restorer, to have it checked over and given an extra polish — he guessed it would be grubby after its brief trip down to Britland.

Wizard Spit and his helper Wizard Polish unwrapped it carefully. 'Odd,' remarked Wizard Spit. 'This isn't the cloth it's usually kept in.'

'It's got a lot of earth on it,' said Wizard Polish, 'as if someone had buried it.'

'And it seems to have been scratched,' said Wizard Spit. 'The Worshipful Wizard won't be pleased. Let's see if we can rub the scratches out.'

'Wait a minute,' said Wizard Polish. 'These aren't scratches. They're writing. Britland writing.'

'What do they say?' asked Wizard Spit. 'I don't understand Britlandish as easily as I used to. Read it aloud, there's a good fellow.'

'What it says,' answered Wizard Polish, carefully examining the round shiny object, is, ' "The Barty Treasure. Donated by Her Grace the Duchess of Barty. May The Best Village Win." Now who on earth would want to write that on the Worshipful Wizard's Crystal Ball?'

'Good gracious,' said Mr Majeika, looking at the ancient car which Mr Potter had pushed out of his garage. 'What on earth is this chariot?'

'This,' answered Mr Potter proudly, giving the headlamps a dust with his handkerchief, 'is the Barty Beauty in which the good folk of Much Barty go hunting each year for the Barty Treasure.'

'How wonderful!' exclaimed Mr Majeika. 'May I ride in it, please, Mr Potter? I'm getting rather good at finding missing treasure.'

Mr Potter frowned. 'It's not altogether regular. By tradition, the Treasure Hunters are Mrs Brace-Girdle and myself. But you are the Teacher In Charge of Treasure-Hunting, so I suppose, just for once, we could squeeze you into the dicky seat, Majeika.'

'Certainly not!' snapped a voice. It was Mrs Brace-Girdle, who had just arrived, dressed to the nines in an antique motoring bonnet and veil. 'Taking an extra passenger could easily disqualify us, Mr Potter. Barty Porcorum may try to break the rules, but we're going to put up a good clean fight.'

'Very well, Bunty,' said Mr Potter humbly. He turned to

Mr Majeika. 'Terribly sorry, Majeika. But maybe you could act as our mechanic – ride alongside us on your . . . er . . . tricycle thing, and change the wheel if we have any trouble.'

'Change the wheel, Mr Potter?' said Mr Majeika eagerly. 'What would you like me to change it into? Or is it like Baby's nappies – do you have to put another one on when it gets wet and dirty?'

'Mr Potter,' snapped Mrs Brace-Girdle, 'I do not intend to take part in this Treasure Hunt if Mr Majeika is anywhere within sight.'

'Yes, Bunty, of course, Bunty,' sighed Mr Potter, rather wishing he hadn't got to spend the day Treasure Hunting with Mrs Brace-Girdle. 'Off you go, Majeika. And off we go! Chocks away!'

He got into the car and looked for the starter-button.

'Surely you remember, Mr Potter,' said Mrs Brace-Girdle icily, 'that a vintage car like the Barty Beauty doesn't have a self-starter. You have to wind the handle.'

Mr Potter turned pale. 'Oh dear, Bunty,' he gasped, 'do I have to go through that again? It's such terribly hard work.'

Mrs Brace-Girdle thought for a moment. 'Very well,' she said. 'Mr Majeika can perform this one task for us. Come on, Mr Majeika, now's your chance! Wind the handle!'

Mr Majeika went to the front of the car and turned the starting handle. Nothing happened. He turned it harder. Still nothing happened. He turned it even harder, and the car suddenly sprang into life. Roaring backwards rather than forwards, it shot in reverse into the garage, ending against the back wall with a loud thump.

Mrs Brace-Girdle gave an angry scream. 'Now see what you've done, Mr Majeika! Ruined the Barty Beauty!'

'No, no,' interrupted Mr Potter, 'it wasn't his fault, Bunty.

It was mine — I must have put the car in reverse gear instead of forward.' He tried to move the gear lever. 'I can't do anything with it,' he said. 'It's stuck in reverse. Wait a minute — there's a note pinned to the dashboard. *"What a beautiful start for Much Barty! You won't find the Treasure in your garage, you silly old Bartyites. Porcorum for ever."* How very unpleasant — whoever could have done such a thing, tampered with the car and left this horrid note?'

Mr Majeika peered at the note. 'I recognize that hand-writing, Mr Potter,' he said. 'It's Hamish Bigmore's.'

'Off we go, then!' shouted Flying Officer Pongo, as Barty Porcorum's own vintage car, the Porcorum Peerless, sped towards the Barty Woods. Hamish was in the back seat, still stuffing chocolates, while in the front, trying to dab oil off her dress with a handkerchief, moped Peaches Popplewell.

'Did you remember to set up the booby traps?' called Flying Officer Pongo over his shoulder.

'Yup,' answered Hamish.

'The buckets full of filthy water that'll pour over them when they drive into the Woods, soaking everyone in the car?'

'Yup,' said Hamish.

'Where's the first booby trap?' called Flying Officer Pongo.

'Here,' answered Hamish, as the Porcorum Peerless struck a trip wire stretched across the road and a bucket full of filthy ice-cold water cascaded all over Peaches.

'The toad!' she screamed. 'The little *toad!*'

*

'We have something serious to report, Your Worshipfulness,' reported Wizard Spit anxiously on the Walpurgian intercom. 'The Crystal Ball isn't the Crystal Ball.'

'Eh? What?' spluttered the Worshipful Wizard, at the other end of the intercom. 'What do you mean, isn't the Crystal Ball?'

'It's something quite like it, Your Worshipfulness, but it's not a Crystal Ball at all. It's some sort of Britland artefact.'

'Majeika's made a mess of things again,' grumbled the Worshipful Wizard. 'Chuck it back to him, and tell him to find the proper one, or he'll have to spend a week in solitary confinement in Outer Darkness. At this rate we'll never be able to have our celebratory party.'

'You've done a wonderful job, Majeika,' said Mr Potter gratefully, when Mr Majeika had finished mending the gear-lever. At first he had tried magic, but he quickly discovered that Hamish Bigmore had simply stuck a lot of chewing-gum into the hole where the lever entered the floor of the car. It only took a matter of minutes to remove it so that the Barty Beauty would once again drive in forward gear as well as backwards. 'I really do think, Bunty,' added Mr Potter, 'that we ought to take Majeika with us.'

'Very well,' said Mrs Brace-Girdle unenthusiastically. 'But he'd better behave himself.'

'Thank you, Mrs Brace-Girdle,' said Mr Majeika. 'And I'd like Melanie and Prince Sam to come with us too. There's plenty of room for us all in the back, if we squash up. You never know when they may be useful.'

*

'Well, Hamish,' said Flying Officer Pongo, who had parked the Porcorum Peerless at the foot of a tree with an envelope pinned to it, 'you seem to have done an absolutely top-hole job planting false clues.'

'Yup,' said Hamish through a mouthful of chocolate.

'You say that when they read the clues in your envelopes, they'll be sent off in a totally wrong direction?'

'Yup,' said Hamish.

'Jolly good show,' said Flying Officer Pongo. 'And what did you do with the real clues, Hamish? The ones we need if we're going to find the Treasure ourselves?'

There was silence from the back seat.

'Don't tell me,' said Peaches Popplewell, who had given up trying to squeeze the filthy water out of her dress, or to dry her mud-spattered hair, 'let me guess. He threw them all away.'

No answer came from Hamish.

'You didn't really, Hamish?' asked Flying Officer Pongo unbelievingly. 'You weren't so stupid, so addle-headed, so bone-brained, that when you were planting the false clues you tore up the real ones without reading them, so that we have absolutely no idea where to find the Barty Treasure?'

Still no answer came from Hamish.

'What did I tell you?' spluttered Peaches Popplewell. 'The toad, the enormous, the absolutely gigantic, the completely and utterly idiotic TOAD!'

'He says what?' asked Wizard Polish.

'He says we've got to chuck this one down to Majeika and get him to throw up the real one,' said Wizard Spit.

'And how are we supposed to spot Majeika, miles and

miles down there in Britland?' sighed Wizard Polish. 'Just tell me that!'

Wizard Spit thought for a moment. 'I suppose,' he said, 'that if we look carefully, we might at least see the real Crystal Ball gleaming in the sun, even if we can't find Majeika.'

He and Wizard Polish began to peer through the trapdoor that led down to Britland.

'Good gracious,' said Mr Potter, as they drove into the Barty Woods. 'What a mess! An empty bucket tied to a rope and lots of bits of paper torn up.'

'Probably townspeople having a picnic and forgetting the Country Code,' snapped Mrs Brace-Girdle.

'If you ask me, Mummy,' said Melanie, 'it's the sort of mess that gets left by Hamish Bigmore. Oh, look!'

The Porcorum Peerless was parked under a tree and Hamish Bigmore was sitting in the back of it. Flying Officer Pongo was shouting furiously at him and Peaches Popplewell seemed to be about to hit him with her handbag. As they watched, Hamish climbed out of the car and ran off through the trees, pursued by Pongo and Peaches.

'Dear me,' said Mr Potter. 'What can be going on? It looks as if the opposition has lost interest in the Treasure Hunt. And goodness, isn't that the Treasure Flag over there, in that clearing?'

He pointed at a small flag stuck in the ground, a short distance away.

They all got out of the Barty Beauty and went over to look. 'Yes, this is it all right,' said Mrs Brace-Girdle. 'Hand me the spade, Mr Majeika, and we'll dig it up.'

Mr Majeika had gone rather white. 'You mean, Mrs Brace-

Girdle, that this is where the Barty Treasure was buried?'

'*Is* buried, Mr Majeika,' answered Mrs Brace-Girdle. 'Clearly we are the first to reach the finishing post, so it must still be here.'

'And is the Barty Treasure round and shiny, Mrs Brace-Girdle,' asked Mr Majeika, even more anxiously, 'and does it look rather like a Crystal Ball?'

'Certainly it does, Mr Majeika,' answered Mrs Brace-Girdle. 'Now, if you would hurry up and get the spade from the car, we can dig it up before our rivals come back.'

'I'm afraid it's too late, Mrs Brace-Girdle,' said Mr Majeika in a whisper.

'Too late? What on earth do you mean?'

'I've dug it up already, Mrs Brace-Girdle, and thrown it into the sky.'

'You've *what*?'

'I think I've spotted it,' said Wizard Polish. 'And I reckon I can see Majeika. Now, take careful aim.'

Wizard Spit took careful aim and chucked the Barty Treasure through the trapdoor.

'I'm sorry, Mrs Brace-Girdle,' Mr Majeika was gasping. 'It won't happen again.'

'Of course it won't,' said Mrs Brace-Girdle furiously. 'And neither will the Barty Treasure Hunt. You, Mr Majeika, have managed to bring to an end one of the great events in our village life. You ought to be ashamed of yourself. You ought —'

'Ow!' said Mr Potter. Something had hit him hard on the back of his head.

'That's it!' called Sam. 'It's come back again, Mr Majeika. They've thrown it down again.'

'Ow!' said Mr Majeika. Something else had hit *him* hard on the head too.

'And there's the Crystal Ball!' said Melanie. 'It must have been stuck in the trees and the Barty Treasure has dislodged it. Chuck it back to Walpurgis as quick as you can, Mr Majeika, and give Mummy the Treasure. Then everyone will be happy!'

Mr Majeika did as he was told.

'I don't know what on earth is going on,' said Mrs Brace-Girdle.

'And neither do I,' said Mr Potter cheerfully. 'But it appears that, after all, Much Barty has won the Barty Treasure Hunt, despite the efforts of Hamish Bigmore to sabotage it, and very much thanks to the help of Mr Majeika. So I think we should all adjourn to School Cottage for a slap-up celebration meal!'

Up in the sky, the Worshipful Wizard was looking happy at last. 'It's back, you say? And Majeika's sent the right one this time? Hooray! That means we can have our party!'

6

FANGS FOR THE
MEMORY

It was a wild and stormy night in Much Barty. Terrible forks of lightning rent the sky, and dreadful claps of thunder shook the ground. Mr Majeika's windmill was lashed by the rain and shaken from side to side by the howling winds. Inside, Mr Majeika crouched cowering in a corner, covering his ears.

In the main street of Much Barty, the rain soaked the flags that had been hung up for the latest village festivity, and made the lettering run on the banner that read 'HAPPY EMPIRE DAY'.

The trees were shaken by the storm, even the great oaks that stood by the village green. A mighty branch of one of them creaked and groaned as the wind bent it from side to side. Finally, with a terrible rending sound, it crashed to the ground.

As it fell, it knocked into a stone statue that stood on the edge of the village green: a statue of an elderly, severe-looking man, which for many years had gazed unblinkingly at the goings-on in Much Barty. The branch hit the statue's head, and knocked it off. The head fell and shattered into a thousand pieces.

And still the storm raged on.

'That'll do very nicely,' said the Worshipful Wizard, upstairs in Walpurgis. 'A touch of forked lightning now, I think, and then a few more thunderclaps, and that's it.'

He waved his magic wand just like a conductor making an orchestra play louder or softer. Indeed, that was exactly what he was doing. All over Walpurgis, posters advertised: 'STORM CONCERT TONIGHT. At 8pm sharp the Worshipful Wizard will conduct his favourite piece, "Thunder and Lightning Over Britland". With rain effects specially provided by Wizard Sprinkler and the Hosepipes. Don't be late!'

There was much applause from the assembled Wizards and Witches as the Worshipful Wizard put down his wand and the storm came to an end. 'Encore! Encore!' they cried eagerly, but the Worshipful Wizard shook his head. 'Not tonight, ladies and gentlemen,' he said. 'I hope to arrange a repeat performance in a week or so, but I think the good people of Britland should now be allowed to sleep in peace. Anyway, there may be some storm damage to repair.'

There was indeed some storm damage — not just in Britland, but in a remote corner of Walpurgis, where a group of stone slabs marked the resting places of sundry demons, ghouls and other creatures of the night, who (thank Walpurgis) spent most of their time sleeping happily in their dark tombs.

One of these slabs had been cracked by the thunderstorm. If the Worshipful Wizard had been there to watch, he would have seen the broken pieces pushed apart from beneath and a head appearing through the gap. An old head, with bloodshot, sunken eyes and, protruding from the mouth, two enormous fangs.

'Where am I?' said the voice of the elderly vampire.

His name was Billy Bloodcup.

After being kept awake by the all-night storm, everyone in Much Barty was surprised to find the morning had dawned bright and clear.

'What splendid weather for the Empire Day festivities, Mr Potter,' said Mrs Brace-Girdle.

'Indeed, Bunty,' responded Mr Potter warmly. 'One of the crowning moments in our St Barty's School year. But I simply can't think what's keeping Majeika.'

What was keeping Mr Majeika at the windmill and making him late for school was his fear of thunderstorms. All through the last night's storm, the tuft of hair in the centre of his head, by means of which he did magic things, had lit up every time there was a flash of lightning, just like a lightning conductor. And he couldn't really believe that the storm had finished.

'Shouldn't you be on your way to school by now, Majeika?' asked the voice of the Worshipful Wizard in his ear.

'B—but the s—storm might s—start ag—gain, Your Worshipfulness,' whispered Mr Majeika.

'No, no,' said the Worshipful Wizard authoritatively. 'The next storm isn't booked until a week's time. We're doing the 1812 Overture and the Royal Fireworks Music then, so it should be a splendid display. But there's a week of fine weather to come before that. Now, off you go.'

Reassured, Mr Majeika triked happily off to school, while up in Walpurgis the Worshipful Wizard peered contentedly down at the clear summer skies. Yes, there was a nice fine day ahead for Majeika. And a nice restful day ahead for himself, making out a Weather Report on last night's storm and planning the next one.

Just then there was a tap on his shoulder. 'Excuse, me, Your Worshipfulness.' It was Wizard Tidings, the Walpurgian bringer of news, both good and bad (usually bad).

'Yes, Wizard Tidings?' asked the Worshipful Wizard.

'I thought you ought to know, Your Worshipfulness, that the vibrations from last night's Storm Concert have dislodged one of the slabs in the Burial Ground and the occupant of the damaged tomb is nowhere to be seen.'

'You mean he's climbed out of his grave, Wizard Tidings?'

'Exactly so, Your Worshipfulness.'

The Worshipful Wizard sighed. Some of these graveyard fellows could be a dratted nuisance when they escaped (as they sometimes did). Wizards don't like to be haunted by ghosts and bothered by skeletons, any more than do Britlanders.

'Who is it this time, Wizard Tidings?' asked the Worshipful Wizard. 'Geoffrey the Ghoul, or Nigel the Nameless Terror, or Douglas the Dreadful, or Kenneth the Creep, or ...' and he named the most fearsome occupant of the Burial Ground, the very sight of whom could strike terror into the heart of every Walpurgian (even though she was really incapable of harming a fly), '... is it Mad Margaret the Iron Maiden?'

'No,' said Wizard Tidings, 'it's none of them. I'm afraid it's Billy Bloodcup.'

'Oh, bother,' said the Worshipful Wizard. 'It would be Billy Bloodcup!'

*

'Happy Empire Day, Mr Potter!' said Mr Majeika as he arrived at school. Triking through the village, he had spotted the Empire Day banner, so that for once he knew what special day it was going to be at St Barty's. 'What do we do on Empire Day, Mr Potter?' he asked eagerly.

'Oh, we wave flags and march about, Majeika,' answered Mr Potter rather gloomily. 'It's much like the other festivities in the school calendar, you know.'

'Is something wrong, Mr Potter?' asked Mr Majeika, concerned that the headmaster did not seem his usual lively self.

'Since you ask, Majeika, yes, there is. It's my poor old uncle.'

'Your poor old uncle, Mr Potter?' asked Mr Majeika. 'Whats happened to your poor old uncle?'

'He's lost his head, Majeika.'

'Lost his head? Oh, Mr Potter, I'm always losing my head and rushing round the place in a terrible muddle, not knowing what I should do next. I expect he'll calm down soon.'

'No, no, Majeika. I mean that his head has fallen off.'

'Fallen off, Mr Potter?' said Mr Majeika, horror-struck. 'How ever did it happen?'

'It was during the storm,' explained Mr Potter. 'He was struck by the branch of a tree.'

'But this is terrible, Mr Potter. I suppose nothing can be done for him?'

'Not a thing, Majeika. We could have used cement, but the head was smashed to pieces.'

'Cement, Mr Potter? Is that what they use in Britland hospitals? And how old was your uncle when this terrible thing happened?'

'Oh, they only put him up last year, Majeika, and one of

his hands fell off as soon as he was erected. But we thought we'd got him good and secure now, so it's been a sad blow.'

Mr Majeika sat down, feeling faint. 'Mr Potter,' he said, 'your uncle seems to have been a very extraordinary person.'

'Oh, he was, Majeika, he was. A great benefactor of the village. He paid for the building of the Village Hall and he gave a lot of money to St Barty's School. So when he died, back in 1895 – '

'1895, Mr Potter?' interrupted Mr Majeika. 'But I thought you said he died last night?'

'As I was saying, Majeika,' went on Mr Potter, 'when he died in 1895, it was planned to erect a statue in his memory. But money was short, and it has taken us more than fifty years to complete the project. The statue of my dear uncle was unveiled only last year, and now, so soon, disaster has struck!'

'A *statue*, Mr Potter? Oh, I see,' said Mr Majeika and began to laugh.

'I don't know what you're laughing at, Majeika,' said Mr Potter, frowning. 'It's a very serious matter.'

'It's a very serious matter,' said the Worshipful Wizard, frowning. 'Last time Billy Bloodcup got loose, there was a dreadful amount of trouble. After all, he is a Vampire.'

'True, Your Worshipfulness,' said Wizard Tidings, 'but remember, he doesn't suck blood. He's a Vegetarian Vampire.'

'As I recall,' said the Worshipful Wizard, 'that didn't make things any better. In fact it made them far, far worse. No Walpurgian objects to letting an ordinary common-or-garden Vampire drink a drop or two of his blood if it's a cold night and the poor creature needs warming up. But this Vegetarian nonsense, as I recall, caused an awful lot of bother.'

'An awful lot,' agreed Wizard Tidings. 'The trouble is, Your Worshipfulness, once types like Billy Bloodcup get out of their graves, it's terribly hard to coax them back. They're like Britland children at the seaside — they just don't want to go home. And you can't really blame them.'

'I suppose not,' said the Worshipful Wizard. 'But a grave is where a Vampire belongs, Vegetarian or not. Somehow or other, you must find Billy Bloodcup and coax him back into his own tomb. At any price.'

Half an hour later, Wizard Tidings saw a ragged old figure slouching along under the walls of the Worshipful Wizard's Residence. 'Got you!' he hissed, grabbing hold of it.

'Ouch, leggo!' screamed the elderly vampire. 'You Wizzes are always moving a poor feller on, when he's done no harm to anyone.'

'Back to your grave, Billy Bloodcup,' said Wizard Tidings firmly.

'Why should I?' grumbled Billy Bloodcup.

'Because that's the rule,' answered Wizard Tidings.

Billy Bloodcup began to snivel. 'But just think, Mister Wizard, when do you suppose I last saw me relatives?'

'Relatives, Billy Bloodcup? Have you got relatives?'

'Of course I has, Mister Wiz, just like any other creature. Why, somewhere around this place is me own Nephew My-Cheeky, as wise and good a Wizard as were ever seen in Walpurgis. Won't you let me free for a day longer, Mister Wiz, so's I can find my Nephew My-Cheeky, what I hasn't seen in a hundred years or more?'

'My-Cheeky?' echoed Wizard Tidings, puzzled. 'I don't

know any Wizard of that name. Wait a moment, do you by any chance mean Majeika?'

'That's it!' cried Billy Bloodcup, his blood-red eyes lighting up as if torches had been switched on behind them. 'My little Nephew My-Cheeky! What a splendid little boy he was when I last saw him.'

'Well, he's not a little boy any more,' said Wizard Tidings. 'He's a full-grown Wizard, or rather, a Failed Wizard, and I'm sorry to say he's been banished down to Britland.'

This news, far from disappointing Billy Bloodcup, seemed to excite him greatly. 'Britland, Mister Wiz? Why, if that isn't the very place I've always wanted to be visiting. Surely His Worshipfulness will grant me a temporary Exit Visa, on grounds of personal hardship, to pop down for a day to Britland to see my dear little Nephew My-Cheeky once again? If he does that, I'll get straight back in my tomb again, promise I will.'

'Melanie! Sam!' called Mr Majeika across the playground. They both came running.

'Yes, Mr Majeika?' they asked.

'You know we've got a Pottery and Plasticine class today? Well, I thought we'd use the occasion to make a new uncle for Mr Potter.'

'A new uncle, Mr Majeika?' asked Melanie, astonished.

'That's right,' said Mr Majeika. 'His last one fell to pieces in the storm, so I thought he'd be terribly pleased if we made a new one for him. It could be unveiled this afternoon, as part of Empire Day. I'll ask the Worshipful Wizard to make sure the weather is fine.'

*

'It seems a most irregular request,' said the Worshipful Wizard, when Wizard Tidings told him that Billy Bloodcup wanted to go down to Britland for the day. 'But as it happens, I might agree to grant it. I just had a call from Majeika. He was asking for specially fine weather today, because he says they're having something called Vampire Day.'

'Vampire Day?' said Wizard Tidings in surprise.

'I know. It doesn't sound like the sort of thing they usually do down there. But I'm sure he said Vampire Day – I couldn't possibly have imagined it. So if it's Vampire Day, why don't we send them a real Vampire?'

After Class Three had done an hour's work at Pottery and Plasticine, it became obvious that the replacement for Mr Potter's uncle was not going to be ready by the afternoon. 'Never mind,' said Mr Majeika. 'There's quite enough happening today as it is. Let's take our time, and finish the job properly tomorrow.'

'Whose head are you going to use, Mr Majeika?' asked Melanie.

Mr Majeika looked round at everyone's attempts to make a head for the statue. None of them would possibly do for Mr Potter's uncle. 'I think we may have to start again,' he said. 'Meanwhile we must hurry down to the village green, or we'll be late for the Empire Day celebrations.'

On the green, Mr Potter was organizing the children into groups. Each of them was clutching a little Union Jack on a stick. 'Excuse me, Mr Potter,' asked Mr Majeika, 'but what exactly is it that Britlanders celebrate on Empire Day?'

'Why, er,' said Mr Potter, slightly at a loss for words,

'we – we celebrate what this country has given to the world, Majeika.'

'And what exactly is that, Mr Potter?'

'Why, er,' said Mr Potter, scratching his head, 'marmalade, don't you know, and ... er ... cricket. You've eaten marmalade, haven't you, Majeika?'

'I'm not sure,' said Mr Majeika. 'But I've certainly eaten crickets. Lovely crisp little green things – they taste delicious on toast.'

Prince Sam pulled Mr Majeika's arm and whispered in his ear. Mr Majeika looked anxiously into the sky.

'What's the matter?' asked Melanie, who could see that something was afoot.

For answer, Mr Majeika pointed a finger skywards. A black balloon was slowly descending towards Much Barty and someone was holding on to the string beneath it.

'A visitor from Walpurgis!' breathed Melanie. 'You weren't expecting anyone, were you, Mr Majeika?'

Mr Potter had drifted off to stop Hamish Bigmore poking a small boy in the face with his flag, so he didn't see Mr Majeika turn pale as he watched the descending figure get nearer and nearer.,

'I hope I'm wrong,' whispered Mr Majeika, 'but that looks horribly like my Uncle Billy.'

'Seems we made a mistake,' said the Worshipful Wizard.

'A mistake, Your Worshipfulness?' asked Wizard Tidings anxiously.

'Majeika has just been on the line, complaining about us sending down his Uncle Billy. Apparently it isn't Vampire Day at all. It's Empire Day, whatever that means.'

'Oh, dear,' said Wizard Tidings.

'Never mind,' said the Worshipful Wizard. 'I don't expect the Britlanders will notice the odd Vampire wandering around. And anyway, he is Majeika's uncle, so Majeika can jolly well cope with him for a day or two. You know what they say about blood being thicker than water.'

'And where a Vampire is concerned,' said Wizard Tidings, 'I should think the blood would be very thick indeed.'

'Quite so,' said the Worshipful Wizard. 'Though of course he is a Vegetarian Vampire.'

'Don't you worry, Nephew My-Cheeky,' squeaked Billy Bloodcup, as he sat in Mr Majeika's favourite armchair. 'I 'asn't bitten a good Neck in three 'undred years. I'm a Vegetarian Vampire now. I only eats Things.'

'I see,' said Mr Majeika anxiously, wiping his brow. It had been an awful bother getting his Uncle Billy away from the village green without anyone seeing — anyone except Melanie and Sam, who had helped him smuggle the old Vampire over to the windmill. Once they'd got him there, the children hadn't lingered, as Mr Potter would soon miss them from the Empire Day celebrations. So Mr Majeika was left alone with his uncle. 'What sort of Things do you eat, Uncle Billy?' he asked anxiously.

Billy Bloodcup looked around him with interest. 'Well, Nephew My-Cheeky,' he said, picking up a nice antique chair that stood by the table, 'this'll do for a start.'

When the Empire Day festivities had finished, and school was over for the afternoon, Melanie and Sam hurried round to the windmill to see what was going on. They found Mr

Majeika sitting miserably on the steps with his head in his hands.

'What's the matter?' they asked him.

'The matter,' said Mr Majeika, 'is that my Uncle Billy has eaten me out of house and home.'

'We can run to the village shop, Mr Majeika,' said Sam, 'and get you some more food.'

'It isn't food I'm talking about, Sam,' said Mr Majeika. 'He eats *everything*, you see — everything except people. Just look.' He got up and threw open the front door.

Inside, everything was in ruins. Enormous bites had been taken out of the table and the armchair; there were teeth-marks all over the umbrella-stand, and half a picture that hung over the mantelpiece had disappeared. 'He had that for his tea,' explained Mr Majeika. 'He's just having a snooze in my hammock now — if he hasn't eaten it. Then he's going to start again. It's awful — soon I shall have no home left at all.'

'But couldn't you send him outside, Mr Majeika?' asked Melanie.

'I did,' said Mr Majeika mournfully. 'Look!' He pointed at the base of the windmill, which had been nibbled all round, as if by some vast dinosaur. 'He tried to eat the sails, but they were out of his reach. I just don't know what to do . . . Ssh! Here he comes now. Well, Uncle, did you have a nice sleep?'

'Not too comfy, Nephew My-Cheeky,' squeaked old Uncle Billy Bloodcup. 'A sight too warm this 'ere windmill is, for someone like meself what's used to a draughty old graveyard. What I needs for a good night's sleep tonight is a slab. A nice chilly slab. You'll see to that, won't you?'

Next morning, Mrs Brace-Girdle was up bright and early to

do her shopping. At the butcher's, she was surprised to see a crowd gathered round the window.

'I call it an absolute disgrace,' Miss Haddock was saying. 'We don't allow tramps and riff-raff into the village, and as for letting them sleep *here* . . .'

Bunty Brace-Girdle pushed her way to the front of the crowd. In the middle of the butcher's window, on the marble slab where meat was usually displayed, a very ragged old man lay fast asleep.

Mr Porterhouse the butcher was telephoning the police. 'I can't do a thing with him,' he was explaining. 'I prodded him with my wooden steak-basher, but he just opened one eye, took a look at that there basher, and *ate it all up*. And I don't like the look of his teeth.'

'It's all my fault,' Mr Majeika explained to Melanie and Sam at tea-time. 'I meant to wake up early and fetch him from the butcher's, but I overslept. Nothing would budge him from that window until he saw a lorry going by with a load of timber, which made his mouth water, and he ran out of the shop and after it. Fortunately I found him feeling rather full after chewing his way through the timber yard, and I persuaded him to come back here.'

'Maybe you could get him to eat up the fallen trees in the Barty Woods,' suggested Sam. 'That should occupy him for days.'

'It's not only wood that he likes,' sighed Mr Majeika. 'When my back was turned just now, I found him toasting my slippers in front of the fire, and eating them with a knife and fork. I'm going to have to keep my Spell Book under lock and key, or he'll chew his way through that.'

'Won't the Worshipful Wizard send another black balloon for him?' asked Melanie. 'Don't forget, it's the way you got rid of Wizard Majolica.'

Mr Majeika shook his head sadly. 'That's been the biggest shock of all. I've just been told that they don't want him back in Walpurgis at all. Apparently he had a perfectly good Visa allowing him to come down here, and now they want him to stay. What am I to do?'

Next day, Mr Majeika turned up at school in his pyjamas. 'It's all I've got to wear,' he explained to Sam and Melanie. 'In the night, he ate every scrap of my clothes. I can't go on like this.'

'Ah, Majeika,' said Mr Potter, coming into the classroom. 'In your modelling overalls again, I see? That's excellent, because a little bird has told me that you're very kindly making a replacement head for my poor old uncle. It would be wonderful if we could unveil it this afternoon. You won't fail me, will you?'

'I'll try not to, Mr Potter,' said Mr Majeika miserably. When the headmaster had gone, he stared around the classroom at Class Three's hopeless attempts to make a head for the statue. 'None of these will do,' he said gloomily to Sam and Melanie. 'Will you two have another go, please? I must hurry back to the windmill to try and stop him eating *everything*.'

'I likes it 'ere,' said Uncle Billy Bloodcup. Mr Majeika had found him chewing his way through a window-frame, which was about the only thing left intact in the windmill. 'Yes, I'd like to stay, Nephew My-Cheeky.'

'Oh, would you, Uncle Billy?' groaned Mr Majeika. 'Well, I can't cope with you here.'

'Anywhere in Britland will do, Nephew My-Cheeky. What I really like is somewhere cold and damp, just like me old grave, but with a bit of company, a few folks passing by, to stop me feeling too lonely, Nephew My-Cheeky. See what you can arrange, will you?'

'I'll do my best, Uncle Billy,' sighed Mr Majeika. 'But you can't stay here. I suppose we might try the village graveyard, but I don't think the Vicar will take kindly to a Vampire-in-Residence. Look, Uncle, put this old blanket over your head – No, don't eat it! I don't want anyone to see you – they're still very cross in the village about your sleeping on the butcher's slab. Now, let's go and see what we can find.'

'Well,' said Melanie, as she and Sam surveyed the clay head they had been carefully modelling all afternoon, 'I don't think that's at all bad.'

'Not at all,' agreed Sam. 'It looks very much like the statue on the village green before the head fell off. I think Mr Potter will be very pleased with it. Now, let's get Mrs Fudd to harden it in the oven, then it'll be ready for the unveiling.'

'Oh, you think Mr Potter will be pleased, do you?' said a voice. It was Hamish Bigmore.

'Hamish, go away,' said Melanie. 'Just because the head you've made looks like a Martian with toothache, there's no need to be rude about other people's.'

'I'll give you a Martian with toothache,' snorted Hamish, and pushed Melanie and Sam's head off the table. It fell to the floor and was dented beyond recognition.

'You idiot,' said Sam. 'Now look what you've done!'

*

'So you see,' Melanie explained to Mr Majeika, when they met him on the edge of the village green, 'there isn't a head we can use for the statue and Mr Potter is coming in ten minutes for the unveiling. Whatever are we going to do?'

Mr Majeika shook his head wearily. 'I've no idea,' he said. Then his face changed. 'Yes I have!' he said. And he turned to the figure he was leading behind him, which was covered with a blanket. 'Uncle Billy!' he whispered.

'Yes, Nephew My-Cheeky?'

'You remember what you said, about wanting to live somewhere cold and damp, but with a bit of company, a few people passing by?'

'Yes, Nephew My-Cheeky?'

'Well, Uncle Billy, I think I've found the place for you. Just the very place!' And he twitched his tuft.

Ten minutes later, Mr Potter was congratulating Mr Majeika on the statue's new head. 'I can't say it's a likeness of my uncle,' he said, 'but it's certainly very striking. Especially the teeth.'

'Well, Mr Potter,' said Mr Majeika, 'it may not be like your uncle, but it's certainly very like mine.'

'Really, Majeika?'

'Oh yes, Mr Potter. Very like him indeed. In fact you might say it's drawn from life.'

When Mr Potter had gone, Melanie said: 'But doesn't your Uncle Billy mind being a statue, Mr Majeika?'

Mr Majeika shook his head. 'It's no worse than being confined inside a grave for another hundred years. He can see and hear everything that's going on around him. And though he can't move in the daytime, I suspect that on dark and stormy nights the Worshipful Wizard may let him roam around a bit.'

'And eat your furniture, Mr Majeika?' asked Sam.

Mr Majeika shook his head. 'No, Sam. The one thing about being a statue is that you completely lose your appetite. So I can make myself a new set of furniture and know that it's completely safe from Uncle Billy Bloodcup.'

ON YOUR MARKS

'The last big day, eh, Majeika?' said Mr Potter cheerfully, as Mr Majeika rolled up to school one summer morning on his tricycle.

'Last, Mr Potter?' asked Mr Majeika, puzzled. 'Oh, you mean the last day of term.'

'Yes, Majeika, but not just that. It's also the last time you'll teach Class Three. Or at least *this* Class Three.' He waved a hand to where Melanie, Hamish Bigmore and Prince Sam were running into school.

'But Mr Potter,' gasped Mr Majeika, 'whatever do you mean? What's going to happen to them?'

'Happen to them, Majeika? Ah, time is like an ever-rolling stream, Majeika. The day has come for them all to leave.'

'Leave, Mr Potter? Leave what, Mr Potter?'

'Why, this school, Majeika. They're all growing up, you know, and there comes a time when our little establishment can no longer contain their growing minds and bodies. Ah, youth,' mused Mr Potter, waxing lyrical, 'youth's a stuff will not endure. Shakespeare said that, Majeika, and he knew a thing or two. Yes, Majeika, it's time for them to depart to make pests of themselves at – I mean, to do their best at – a bigger and even more time-hallowed educational institution. The males of the species, Majeika, are passing on to the legendary Bartminster College for Boys, while the girls go to Bartminster Ladies'. Those who pass their exams, that is.'

'Is Bartminster a really famous school, Mr Potter?' asked Mr Majeika.

'Indeed it is, Majeika. It has produced no less than five Prime Ministers, eight Archbishops and the fashion editor of the *Barty Bugle*.'

'And what about those who don't pass their exams, Mr Potter?' asked Mr Majeika anxiously, remembering his own punishment after failing the Sorcery Exams. 'They're not . . . banished?'

Mr Potter blinked. 'Not exactly, Majeika. But they have to find places where they can, at other, less distinguished seats of education. Yes, Majeika, it's a testing time for all of them. None of us, whether pupil or teacher, can hear the word "Examina tions" without at least a faint quiver of nerves.'

'Examinations,' grumbled the Worshipful Wizard, up in Walpurgis. 'Surely it's not time for the Examinations yet again, Wizard Marks?'

Wizard Marks, a sharp-featured wizard who always carried a clipboard and a very pointed pencil, nodded stiffly. 'It most certainly is, Your Worshipfulness. We have a whole batch of young Wizards and Witches ready to sit Sorcery and Spells for the first time, and of course certain individuals who failed last time are allowed to try again.'

'Oh, well,' sighed the Worshipful Wizard, 'let's get on with it. Who are the candidates this year, Marks?'

Wizard Marks drew breath and read out a long list of

names. At the end, he said: 'So may I present you with the list for your official signature, Your Worshipfulness?'

The Worshipful Wizard, who had almost fallen asleep during the recital of names, took the clipboard and pencil from Wizard Marks, and was about to sign when something occurred to him. 'I can't see Majeika's name on this list,' he said.

'Majeika?' answered Wizard Marks, frowning. 'No, we've no one of that name.'

'But you remember Majeika, don't you, Marks?'

'Only vaguely, Your Worshipfulness. If you could remind me . . .?'

'Little chap with big specs, a check suit and a mop of hair with a tuft in the middle. After he'd failed seventeen times we sent him down to Britland, to be a teacher.'

'Oh, him,' said Wizard Marks, smiling unpleasantly. 'Yes, of course, Your Worshipfulness. But you're not seriously suggesting that we give him another chance? I mean, Your Worshipfulness, seventeen times . . .'

'Maybe,' said the Worshipful Wizard. 'But he's served his sentence faithfully in Britland, doing what most Failed Wizards have to do when we send them down there.'

'Being a Traffic Warden?' asked Wizard Marks.

'No, no, a Teacher. He's worked hard at teaching and I really do think we ought to give him another chance.'

'But if I recall aright,' said Wizard Marks, tight-lipped, 'last time he scored the lowest ever achieved by any candidate. Nought out of a hundred in Spells Practical, and minus two for Spells Biological, before knocking down the entire Witches' Knitting Circle during his Broomstick Flying Test. Do you really believe such a person is worthy of one more chance, Your Worshipfulness?'

'I do, Wizard Marks. I really do.'

Wizard Marks pursed his lips crossly. 'If it pleases Your Worshipfulness. But you must understand, Your Worshipfulness, that a candidate with such a bad track-record as Majeika will need to satisfy the examiners at a higher level than usual before we would be willing to admit him to the ranks of Qualified Wizards.'

'You mean you're going to make the questions harder for him?'

Wizard Marks nodded. 'And of course, in the event of his eighteenth failure, we would have to apply the ultimate punishment.'

'You mean . . .?' asked the Worshipful Wizard.

Wizard Marks nodded again. The Worshipful Wizard sighed. 'You're a hard man, Marks. I suppose you're right. I'm sure Majeika would like to attempt the exams again. But clearly this is going to be his last chance . . .'

'I just can't believe it,' said Pam Bigmore emotionally. 'My own Hamish, my very own little boy, off to big school at last!' She was driving Hamish in the family Rolls Royce to Bartminster School, where he was to be interviewed by the Headmaster for a place next autumn. 'Oh, Hamie,' said Pam, 'Mummy and Daddy are going to be so proud of you.'

On the back seat, Hamish blew a big bubble of bubblegum.

'The Head will see you now,' said the grey-haired butler when they arrived at Bartminster. Pam Bigmore looked around at the ivy-clad towers, the great playing-fields with their goal-posts and the tall chapel built of mellow Bartyshire stone. 'Ah, Bartminster,' she sighed. 'You don't know how lucky you are to have my Hamie as a pupil. Take out your bubble-gum, Hamish, there's a good little boy.'

Hamish took out his bubble-gum and stuck it on the door of the Headmaster's study.

They went in and sat down. The Headmaster, a tall distinguished-looking man, was sitting behind his desk. He put on his glasses and looked carefully at Hamish.

Hamish stuck out his tongue.

The Headmaster sighed deeply. 'Quite frankly, Mrs Bigmore,' he said, 'we have very few places on offer at the moment. And whom we choose out of all the applicants depends a great deal – a very great deal – on the boy's behaviour at interview.'

Pam Bigmore leant over and tapped Hamish on the shoulder. 'D'you hear that, Hamish? The Headmaster says it all depends on the interview.'

Hamish took some more bubble-gum out of his pocket and put it in his mouth. 'That's OK,' he said, pointing at the Headmaster. 'He's passed the interview. Now, when do I start?'

The Headmaster shook his head gravely. 'I'm afraid, Mrs Bigmore, that your son is under a slight misapprehension. It is *I* who have to approve *him*, not the other way round. And besides, we still have the Common Entrance Examination to consider.'

Pam Bigmore blushed angrily. 'Who are you calling common?' she snapped.

'What's the matter, Mr Majeika?' said Melanie after lunch. 'You look worried.'

'I am,' sighed Mr Majeika. 'I've just had a call from the

Worshipful Wizard. They're summoning me back to Walpurgis to sit my Sorcery Exams all over again.'

'For the eighteenth time?' asked Prince Sam.

Mr Majeika nodded. 'And if I fail this time, I really will be banished.'

'Back here, to go on teaching?' asked Melanie.

'No, Melanie, far worse than that. I shall be stripped of all magic powers, and banished to the patch of damp ground behind Walpurgis to spend the remaining years of my life as a Fourth-Class Broomstick Mender.'

'How awful,' said Melanie. 'But couldn't you just refuse to take the exams again, and stay here to teach Class Three?'

'I suppose I could, couldn't I?' said Mr Majeika, his face brightening up. Then it fell again. 'But *you* won't be here, Melanie, nor you, Sam, nor anyone from the Class Three I know. It won't be the same at all.'

'Oh yes it will, Mr Majeika,' said a voice. It was Hamish Bigmore. 'I'll still be here,' said Hamish, grinning.

'You, Hamish?' asked Mr Majeika, astonished. 'But I thought you were going on to Bartminster with the other boys?'

Hamish Bigmore shook his head. 'They won't have me,' he said cheerfully. 'My mum had almost persuaded the Head to take me, but then he saw the rude words I'd written on the exam papers.' He gave a gleeful laugh. 'And they won't take me at any of the other seventeen schools my mum has tried. So Mr Potter has agreed to keep me here and I can have special teaching.'

'Special teaching, Hamish?' asked Mr Majeika. 'Who's going to give you that?'

'Ah, Majeika,' said Mr Potter, joining the group. 'Have you heard young Hamish's news? He's not leaving St Barty's

117

after all. He's staying here, probably for years and years and years. Isn't that splendid?' Mr Potter's face began to twitch.

'So who is going to teach him, Mr Potter?' asked Mr Majeika.

'Well, Majeika,' began Mr Potter, 'I rather thought that you . . .'

'That settles it,' Mr Majeika whispered to Melanie and Sam. 'Being a Broomstick Mender would be better than teaching Hamish for the rest of my life. I'm sorry, Mr Potter,' he said to the headmaster, 'but even though Hamish isn't leaving, I am. I've been offered the opportunity of obtaining a higher qualification.'

Mr Potter blinked. 'Congratulations, Majeika. But this puts me in a difficult position. Where on earth am I going to find someone else to teach Hamish Bigmore?'

'Wizard Marks?' said the Worshipful Wizard, on the Walpurgian intercom system.

'Yes, Your Worshipfulness?' answered the voice of Wizard Marks.

'I've had a complaint, Wizard Marks. From a certain Apprentice Wizard Spex, who was banished to Britland in 1903.'

'Ah yes, Your Worshipfulness. I think I recall the case.'

'He says he's never been invited back to sit the Sorcery Exams again, in all these years.'

'Well, Your Worshipfulness,' answered Wizard Marks, 'he is blind as a bat, or at least extremely short-sighted. Hence his name, Your Worshipfulness. He was quite unable to read the exam papers last time.'

'But do you know what Wizard Spex's job has been, all these years in Britland, Wizard Marks?'

'A teacher, like Majeika, sir?'

'No. Wizard Spex has been working as an optician. He makes glasses for people. So presumably by now he's equipped himself with a pair, which means that this time he'll be able to see the exam papers properly. Send for him, Wizard Marks.'

In a small street in the town of Bartminster, not far from the famous boys' school, stood a small shop, with a signboard that read 'W. SPEX. OPTICIAN.'

Inside, an old man with a long white beard and an enormous pair of glasses was peering short-sightedly at an invitation card which had just arrived by black balloon that morning. It was, of course, a message from Walpurgis.

Just to make sure that Wizard Spex understood it, the Worshipful Wizard had ordered that the summons be set out as an optician's eye-test card:

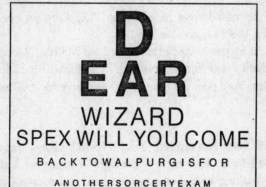

'D – E – A – R,' read the old man with difficulty. 'That spells "dear". Can't make out the rest of it. I wonder what they want?' So when the black balloon came for him, he was quite surprised.

Mr Majeika had declined the offer of a black balloon to take him up to Walpurgis; he said he would much rather make the journey on his trike. He was just saying goodbye to Melanie and Sam when Mr Potter came round the corner.

'Off already, Majeika?' asked Mr Potter. 'How are you going? By Piggy Wilson's taxi to the station, or maybe by bus?'

'Not exactly, Mr Potter,' said Mr Majeika. At that moment the trike came round the corner by itself, excitedly ringing its bell. It was looking forward to the journey back to Walpurgis.

Mr Potter gazed at it in astonishment, and rubbed his eyes. 'Dear, dear, I obviously need a good rest. It gets to us all in the end, Majeika.' And he walked off, muttering to himself. 'I still haven't found anyone to teach Hamish Bigmore,' he called over his shoulder. 'Do keep an eye out, Majeika, there's a good fellow.'

'I'll do my best, Mr Potter,' called Mr Majeika. 'Goodbye, and thank you for everything.' He turned to Melanie and Sam. 'And now it's time to say goodbye to you,' he said sadly.

'Wizard Spex has arrived, Your Worshipfulness,' reported Wizard Marks. 'He's more short-sighted than ever, but he's sitting waiting in the examination hall, so I suppose we've got to give him a chance.'

'Then get it over with, Marks,' instructed the Worshipful Wizard.

'We can't start yet, sir,' said Wizard Marks. 'Majeika hasn't arrived. Of course, Your Worshipfulness, there are penalties for being late . . .'

'Now don't be unfair, Marks,' said the Worshipful Wizard. 'He's got a lot of goodbyes to say down there. But tell you what, I'll speed things up and bring him up here right away.' He waved his magic wand.

There was a flash and a puff of smoke, and suddenly Mr Majeika on his trike was sitting in front of the Worshipful Wizard. And with him were Melanie and Sam.

'Great galaxies!' spluttered the Worshipful Wizard. 'What are these Britland bratlings doing here, Majeika?'

'Sorry, Your Worshipfulness,' said Mr Majeika, smiling, 'but you gave me absolutely no warning of blast-off. And I was just giving them a goodbye hug, so up they came too. Well, well, children,' he said to them, 'you never thought you'd see the inside of Walpurgis, did you?'

'But this is preposterous, Your Worshipfulness,' snapped Wizard Marks. 'If I may draw your attention to Rule 409, sub-section 3,004 in the *Good Wizards' Guide*, Your Worshipfulness, where it clearly states that no Earthlings are allowed up to Walpurgis.'

'So it does, Wizard Marks, so it does,' said the Worshipful Wizard, smiling. 'But here they are, through nobody's fault, and as they're here they might as well have a look round. Give them a guided tour, Majeika.'

'Oh, may I, sir? Thank you, sir!' said Mr Majeika.

'That was wonderful, Mr Majeika,' said Sam, after they had

visited the Witches' Knitting Circle, the Cauldron Cookery Club and the Creepy Catacombs, and seen all the other delights that Walpurgis had to offer.

'I'm glad you could have a look around,' said Mr Majeika. 'But now I've got those awful exams to face. They should have started half an hour ago, and I know Wizard Marks is in a terrible temper with me, so I'd better hurry into the examination hall.'

'Couldn't we come in and help you, Mr Majeika?' said Melanie.

'Not allowed, I'm afraid, Melanie. I've simply got to do it on my own.'

Wizard Marks had arranged special papers for Mr Majeika and Wizard Spex, who sat together in a corner of the examination hall. Mr Majeika was afraid that Wizard Marks had decided to make them even harder than usual.

Wizard Marks stood in front of the two candidates, reading out the questions. 'Question One,' he snapped. 'Wizard Oz has 720 bats. If he bathes half of them on Thursday, and a quarter of them on Friday, how many bats does Wizard Oz have to bathe on Saturday?'

Mr Majeika held up his hand: 'He doesn't have to bathe any of them, sir. Any properly qualified Wizard knows that bats hate being bathed. If you need to clean their wings, you just brush them with a soft brush.'

'Be quiet Majeika,' barked Wizard Marks. 'Just write down the answer to the question.'

Miserably, Mr Majeika chewed the end of his pencil, and tried to work out the sum.

'Question Two,' snapped Wizard Marks, long before Mr

Majeika had finished. 'If it takes 140 Witches 17 weeks to make 346 broomsticks, how long does it take 120 Witches to make 253 broomsticks?'

Mr Majeika's hand shot up again. 'But sir, any qualified Wizard knows that Witches don't make broomsticks. They're manufactured by the Broomstick Factory, just beyond the Catacombs.'

'Majeika,' snarled Wizard Marks, 'this is your last warning. If you don't answer the questions I've set, then you will automatically be failed. And you know what will be the consequences of that.'

Outside the examination hall, Melanie and Sam waited anxiously for news. Sam peered through the keyhole. 'They're just beginning Spells Practical,' he said.

'How's Mr Majeika doing?' asked Melanie.

'Dreadfully. He's just turned Wizard Marks into an elephant. I'm sure that wasn't right – the elephant is looking furious.'

'And Wizard Spex?'

'He's laughing his head off at Mr Majeika's mistake. I'm afraid it looks as if he's going to pass and Mr Majeika fail shamefully badly.'

'Time's up!' said a voice behind them. It was the Worshipful Wizard.

Melanie and Sam stood aside as he strode forward importantly, and opened the doors of the examination hall. 'Well then, Marks,' he called, 'what's the result?'

There was no answer, because the elephant, of course, could not speak.

'I'm afraid it's my fault, Your Worshipfulness,' explained

Mr Majeika. 'I've accidentally turned him into an elephant and I can't remember how to turn him back. Just give me a chance, and I'll set things right.'

Wizard Spex began to chortle. 'Oh, you've messed up your chances, Majeika, even I can see that. Turned the examiner into an elephant, ho ho ho! What a silly ass you've been.'

'And what have *you* achieved in Spells Practical, Wizard Spex?' asked the Worshipful Wizard sharply.

'Nothing yet, Your Worshipfulness,' mumbled Wizard Spex. 'My spell didn't seem to do anything at all. But I've got all the answers right so far — you can look at his mark-sheet.' And he pointed at Wizard Marks's clipboard, which lay abandoned on the ground.

'That may be so, Wizard Spex,' said the Worshipful Wizard. 'But the examination rules state clearly that Spells Practical is the essential part of the exam. You may have got one hundred per cent in the written papers, but if you can't pass Spells Practical, then you're out.'

'It's not fair,' grumbled Wizard Spex.

'It's perfectly fair,' answered the Worshipful Wizard. 'What use are Wizards who can do sums if they can't do spells? Now, Wizard Spex, here's your chance. Wizard Majeika has turned Wizard Marks into an elephant. You turn him back into his proper shape.'

Wizard Spex thought for a moment, then he waved his wand.

There was a flash and a puff of smoke, and where the elephant had been there stood a shiny black new tricycle, just like Mr Majeika's.

'You've failed,' said the Worshipful Wizard to Wizard Spex. 'And you,' he said to Mr Majeika, 'have passed.'

'But I wasn't supposed to turn him into an elephant at all,' said Mr Majeika.

'Maybe not,' said the Worshipful Wizard. 'But we've all been trying to turn him into something for years. He's a perfect pest, with his wretched exams – do you know, he tried to make *me* take some exam the other day – said it was a necessary qualification for me to retain my job! We've all been longing to see the back of him for centuries, but try as we could, no spell would change him into anything. And now you've done it, Majeika. You certainly deserve to pass.' He turned to Wizard Spex. 'As for you,' he said, 'I admit you haven't been treated altogether fairly. But what I have in mind for you isn't really so dreadful, as Mr Majeika will confirm. You're going to go straight back to Britland, Spex – as a teacher!' And without more ado he pushed Wizard Spex through the trapdoor that led down to Britland. 'He can take over your old job, Majeika,' he said. As an afterthought, he pushed the new trike through as well.

'And teach Hamish Bigmore!' said Melanie. 'Poor Wizard Spex, he didn't really deserve that.'

'Well, we'll let him stay there a term or two,' said the Worshipful Wizard, 'and then he can have another chance. But it serves him right for laughing when things went wrong for Majeika. And now, Majeika, it's time to invest you with your robes and insignia as a Qualified Wizard.'

'Couldn't we stay just a little bit longer?' asked Melanie an hour or so later, when the Graduation Ceremony was over and Mr Majeika had been installed as a fully-qualified member of the College of Wizards.

'It's wonderful up here,' said Sam. 'I don't want to go back at all.'

'I'm afraid you can't stay any longer, bratlings,' said the Worshipful Wizard. 'All good things have to come to an end.'

'Can't they just stay for the party, sir?' asked Mr Majeika. 'The party is the best bit of all.'

The Worshipful Wizard smiled. 'All right,' he said. 'They can stay for the party.'

And the party went on for the rest of that day, and all night. At the end of it Melanie and Sam were so tired that they scarcely noticed when Mr Majeika said goodbye to them, gave them a hug, and sent them floating gently back to Britland. Next morning they woke up in their own beds, wondering if it hadn't all been a dream.

'Can I ever see them again, sir?' Mr Majeika asked the Worshipful Wizard.

'I expect something can be arranged now and then, Majeika. And in any case,' continued the Worshipful Wizard, smiling, 'remember that though you're a fully qualified Wizard, you're still only a probationer member of the College. And if we find that your spells aren't consistently up to scratch, you'll be blasted back all the way to Britland, Majeika, to do some other job down there. So take care!'